SPRING
OF LIGHT

SPRING
OF LIGHT

RENATO BETTIO

Halo
PUBLISHING
INTERNATIONAL

Halo Publishing International
7550 W IH-10 #800, PMB 2069,
San Antonio, TX 78229

First Edition, February 2025
ISBN: 978-1-63765-732-4
Library of Congress Control Number: 2024926798

The information contained within this book is strictly for informational purposes. Unless otherwise indicated, all the names, characters, businesses, places, events and incidents in this book are either the product of the author's imagination or used in a fictitious manner. Any resemblance to actual persons, living or dead, or actual events is purely coincidental.

Halo Publishing International is a self-publishing company that publishes adult fiction and non-fiction, children's literature, self-help, spiritual, and faith-based books. We continually strive to help authors reach their publishing goals and provide many different services that help them do so. We do not publish books that are deemed to be politically, religiously, or socially disrespectful, or books that are sexually provocative, including erotica. Halo reserves the right to refuse publication of any manuscript if it is deemed not to be in line with our principles. Do you have a book idea you would like us to consider publishing? Please visit www.halopublishing.com for more information.

CONTENTS

Longings 180

THE LIGHT

It had been quite some time since the Light came to town. Its first sighting was somewhat of a surprise, as it was only possible to see it shining on top of the hill, on moonless nights.

The hill was what remained of a dead volcano. To get to its top, one had to walk a thousand meters or so, starting from where Del Calvario Street split, then left on a path that led down to the old *pilas*, where people have washed their clothes since before anyone can remember, and then right on the Marie Pilar Bridge, which crosses the ravine that splits the town in half. Nobody knows why the bridge was originally named that, but now it is known as the María del Pilar Bridge, maybe because it is easier to pronounce.

From the small bridge with decorative balusters and a central archway bearing the carved faces of two young women, the climb was about a thousand meters up side of Chagüite and then skirting a thin river that springs from the top of the hill and opens into the ravine. On its way down, the river creates little waterfalls and pools, which provide amusement for the townsfolk. Close to the top, the traces of the volcano become apparent where, suddenly, at the turn of a corner, hot springs, limestone, clay, and pools of hot water scrape the volcanic rock.

Nobody—not even *las comadres* in the market, who always know essential information—could exactly say when the Light was first seen. There were vague theories about its origin; the elderly swore it predated both radio and TV.

When asked about it, they answered, "Uy! That was here before President Manuel Enrique. My mother says, one night, he climbed the Chagüite; he wanted to know the Light. When he came down, he proclaimed he would run for president."

The Light's fame spread past the town's limits and became known in the capital. One day, a group of soldiers entered the town under orders of Lieutenant Colonel Chebo Monterrosa. At that time, it was legal for a lieutenant colonel to organize a *coup d'état* and become the nation's president.

Once he enlisted as a soldier, Monterrosa couldn't hide that this was his aim. He was a Westerner born to a poor family in a poor town. His ambition drove him to seize control as soon as possible. He enrolled in night school and graduated with honors. After that, he steadily rose in rank and, at thirty-seven, became a lieutenant. The *Diccionario de la Lengua Española de la Real Academia* kept his mind occupied; he memorized random words and incorporated them into his vocabulary with the firm idea that a president must be as sophisticated as possible.

He didn't bother to announce his arrival to the mayor or to the post sergeant of the National Guard, for they were about to be his inferiors and thus must obey him. When he and his troops met at the town's central park, he spoke to them with an affected tone, "Our mission here is as essential as any unforeseen finding that suddenly resolves a mystery, and it requires the same amount of seriousness. The contact with this Light can endow a chosen one with important leadership talents."

As he finished speaking, the soldiers applauded, and he favored them with a grand smile. Then he made his way to the mayor's office, and the soldiers took the opportunity to interrogate Tulio Gavidia, who knew how to read because he had gone to school.

"*Mirá*, Tulio, what does 'require' mean? And what exactly is an 'endow'?"

"'Require' means to quire twice, you know? The lieutenant really wants to see the Light badly enough to try the climb twice. And 'endow,' I heard that's a *cachimbona* fruit that grows only in Guatemala."

That explanation satisfied the soldiers, so they got ready for the climb. For such an important mission, Monterrosa had covered the insides of some *yute* bags with tar, for, if not, he reasoned, the Light might be able to escape through the little holes in the *yute*. The bags had wide openings, and their necks were reinforced with *manta* bands with sewed loops through which a piece of rope, when the bags were filled with the Light, could be cinched tight so that the Light couldn't escape. In Monterroso's mind, the Light would be taken out of the bags handful by handful and distributed amongst those who held his favor when he achieved the presidency. Each soldier would be in charge of two or three bags, opening them wide as soon as they got to the Light and entrapping in each one as much radiance as possible.

The troops arrived on a rainy, dark, and windy midday. They came with the news of flooded rivers, alleys, and valleys in the lower coastal regions. "We are busy," the soldiers answered when the townsfolk tried to dissuade them from climbing the hill with the storm so close.

Close to five o' clock, as the troops reached the María del Pilar Bridge to begin the ascent, the soldiers were already soaking wet; moisture made the bags heavier than they should be. Yet, obedient, they climbed slowly, with the rain worsening at moments and various difficulties arising along the way. The narrow river, now swollen, spilled over its edges. The soldiers' muddy boots made the climb even more difficult, but that didn't dissuade them from reaching the top and taking samples of the Light. This, they thought, would make them better people.

Just when they were about to reach the hot springs, all the fury of the typhoon unloaded on them. The roar was deafening, and the trees began to bend, losing branches to the force of the wind. One of those branches found a soldier's head, felling him in spite of his helmet.

Terror came over the troops, and Monterroso realized his mission was in vain. He told himself, *This wind won't let us bag even a little of the Light.*

As night was already closing in, they began the slow descent, which proved to be as hard as the initial climb. The trails were slippery, and two soldiers fell in the pools, saved only by the bags, which floated. A wounded soldier had to be helped down by one of his colleagues who functioned as his guide and staff.

At midnight, the troops were back in the town's central park. There was not a soul outside. The storm, though greatly deflected by the surrounding mountains, unloaded on the town great streams of rain that descended furiously and puddled and flowed through the streets. The soldiers ate their rations in silence, under cover of the park's kiosk, until their lieutenant gave the order to march to the capital in spite of the gale and the dangers along the road.

In the town, there was further news of Monterroso. At the capital, he had tried to overthrow the government, but he was stopped by rebellious troops still loyal to the president. Monterroso was imprisoned in his natal town's jail until a new president, a friend of his since their recruit years, pardoned him and sent him with his family back to the capital.

It was known amongst the townsfolk that the Light must be approached without violence or ambition, with a mind willing to learn whatever it had to teach. From this belief was born the idea of making pilgrimages to the top of the hill. Based on the different religions of the townsfolk, each church organized their own visitations. Contributions were needed to finance these pilgrimages. The most shameless, abusive, and cunning organizers kept the majority of the money. And up they went, "hoping to reach the Light," aspiring mayors, deputies, governors...

Once, Paco Luna's *marero* friends convinced him to climb the hill. They intended to steal a strand of the Light and sell it for a convenient price to the town's rascals. Paco had just gotten out of prison for stealing a bike, and the *mareros* had told him that if he laid eyes on even the slightest ray of the Light, it would be enough to change his life of cheating.

Paco walked them to a little waterfall, and there he spoke these words so adamantly they could be etched in stone, "I'm staying here. I'm cool; *estoy cachimbón*. I need no light. You go ahead. I'll head back when it pleases me."

Even churches took part in the matter—the Light had turned into an essential element of the townsfolk's life, and they feared it would disrupt or, worse, contradict their religious beliefs.

Fortunately, around that time, a Spanish priest arrived in town and educated them with a great sense of purpose. He explained to the folks in a sermon, "My limited understanding of the Light indicates that it doesn't contradict our faith's dogma."

So this mystery turned profound or banal, depending on each specific conversation. Scholars came from all over the country: university experts on philosophy, physics, chemistry, meteorology, occultism, and more. They all explained the Light phenomenon according to their expertise and in the end formed a National Commission for Light Studies. Books full of arguments that explained the origin of the Light were published, but none of the authors dared even once climb the hill at night to let their spirits contemplate and their nerves feel the presence of the Light.

Years went by; contemplation of the Light, in a town where its radiance was constant and ordinary, became unnecessary. Until THE CONFLICT exploded as eloquently as the blare of a thousand trumpets, a civil war with an insatiable hunger for death, as is its custom. The war killed 75,000 people and victimized 260,000 widows, orphans, and wounded. The town was no exception for the shadow of death. Some confrontations took place in it; one drama unfolded right downtown. After the shooting, the young bodies of men riddled with bullets could be counted on the paths, where they were lined up, surrounded by flower beds.

Someone described the sight in verse, narrating how the remnants of a proud race bled, the Maya Lenka who once called the foothills of the town's mountain home. The poem is still there, framed and hanging on a wall in city hall.

War lasted twelve years and left a profound economic disaster that hurt even the stoic town, which had known poverty since the beginning of its history. Exodus towards the north was imperative for many families who lost loved ones in the conflict. From this exodus, made up of thousands of orphans, would one day rise gang violence in the form of the *maras*.[1] They ravaged the innocence of any young man who refused to join them, they raped young women without consequence, they threatened anyone who refused to pay their bribes, and they delivered on their threats with homicides.

A *gringo* president deported a thousand of these men who knew only violence and exploitation, men who lacked any trace of spirit renewal or consideration for the sanctity

---

[1] Criminal gangs that operate in Central America.

of life, men who were experts on vengeance and leeches on their fellow man. The name of this president was plastered on the corners of one of the main streets until an unsympathetic government came to power and tore down the signs that read his name. They were thrown in the trash. "Where they should be" was the new government's explanation.

It was then that the radiance of the Light intensified.

"Something changed," said the town's elders.

"Let's hope it is for the better," answered the *comadres*, who always know more than they let on.

On a Sunday just like any other, as the afternoon's sun sank, the earth roared. Witnesses recounted it sounded as if a mountain were falling in chunks into an invisible lake. The chaos produced by the phenomenon was terrifying; as soon as the earthquake started, victims had already lost hope of surviving. It lasted nine minutes and destroyed every one of their homes. The church and its bell tower, the pride of the town, were annihilated in an instant, the bell tower almost in midair as the bell fell on an elementary school teacher.

A judge, interrupted at the most crucial moment of his speech, collapsed still in his chair when it fell onto a septic tank that was exposed by the violence of the shaking of the earth. The fall saved the judge's life; afterward, he said that he would never get mad if someone mocked him about the smelly incident.

A thousand died. The military blockade for the removal of the corpses and debris lasted three months. During these days of irreparable loss, the Light's radiance grew brighter than ever before. The hill lit its great guiding torch, warm and hopeful, which was a far greater beacon than misery.

International help was quick and effective. North Americans, as always, donated the most, but, also as always, the help they provided drained into the pockets of the nation's leader. Reconstruction was slow and painful. The Italian and Swedish families who had settled down in town due to the amazing climate and richness of their coffee plantations closed their homes forever and were lost to history. There were valuable exceptions, however: two or three Swedish families and three or four Italian families who stayed to share the town's misfortune.

Reconstruction took six years. Peruvian companies in charge of the renewal did magnificently. Houses were rebuilt with seismic-resistant iron columns and cement blocks, *duralita* sealings and appropriate drainage. All septic tanks were forever sealed, and the availability of utilities like drinkable water and electric lights foresaw a prosperous life.

But great mistakes were also made. The old town's straight streets were replaced by a never-ending curve. Completely demolished was the old central park. It had been commissioned by President Manuel Enrique and was the venue for ceremonies, lovers' encounters, breaking of decorated eggs full of confetti on children's heads on Semana Santa, and afternoon skating on the geometric patterns of the brick pavers.

The varnished bricks were replaced by coarse cement. The gazebo where the municipal band played on weekends, brightening afternoons and nights, was razed and replaced by an inaccessible area with no way in or out. None of this had any explanation, but the townsfolk, grateful for the reconstruction, did not complain. Instead, they surrendered to change.

Years later, after the Civil War and the earthquake, came the gangs. The general character of the national environment gradually changed; new words and new ideas were introduced. They were all part of the young slang: "*la droga*," "*la mara*," so innocently said, almost ignorantly, as if they weren't discussing the virtue of life or the possibility of death. Elders were disrespected notably; television showed images of young *mareros* surrounding older men like wolf packs, shattering them under a barrage of repeated kicks and other humiliations. This was all part of the gang initiations, the tests that must be passed to enter the gangs as loyal members.

The list of murders was never-ending. Going out at night was reckless, no matter where you were in the country. It felt as if criminals had more rights than victims did, and long-term frustration took a toll on the spiritual force of the national soul. There was no rescue in sight; all past and present presidents were unscrupulous, deceitful, fraudulent, lying thieves.

Gustavo Padilla, the town's wise old man, constantly repeated, "There's nothing more despicable than stealing from poor townsfolk."

And yet, there was always somebody doing exactly that with arrogance, cunning, and a knack for excuses and unkept promises. Some of them, after looting the national treasury, bought forged papers to prove they were a neighboring country's nationality to avoid any consequences that would weaken their claims of being honorable. One of them, before leaving the country, unclothed his soul when asked about his crimes, "These dumbasses deserve nothing, man! But me, with my dough…I can rebuy the presidency if I please."

In the town, the Light didn't give any sign of diminishing. Its radiance was even more apparent; it illuminated the hill like a miniature sun. People smiled at the sight; they knew they had something unique that should be preserved for the brave during adversity, for heroes on their quests, for thinkers and poets who foretold events and enriched the universe.

The likelihood of an upheaval was tangible—a protest, a social storm that would straighten the course of the country and resurrect the old history and hope in a town accustomed to pain, eternal hunger, no way out...

That was the state of things. The Light did not move; though, its radiance changed according to the nation's sentiment. It appeared the Light responded to desperation as much as it did to joy and celebration, becoming dimmer on happier days and lush when anguish that needed easing was present. A name was never given to it, for according to the townsfolk, it didn't need one, as everyone knew from where and Whom it came. It required no guards, fences, or walls to keep it safe. Those who were confident and carried themselves with nobility of soul could get close to it. With a little luck, they would descend in the middle of the night with a better understanding of the value of humanity. Astonishingly, those minds desperate for an explanation of the origin of the Light would never be able to find the simple wisdom it took to approach it.

Finally, what was anticipated arrived: what the nation required to calmly walk into the conversation of the free folk. No more tyranny, no more theft, no more corruption of justice, no more fear when walking the streets in the middle of the night, no more hunger for the little ones in schools. We were ready to learn what was new and to respect what was old and smelled of eternity; ready to make out in the distance a long, wide horizon; ready to light up the roads with laughter; ready to incorporate into our lives the constant impression that things could suddenly change, ready to feel that the only solution lies within ourselves, based on truth and not crime, arrogance, and insult, not on the shameless theft of the country's meager resources.

The Light remained unchanged. Its meaning couldn't be guessed at. Why had it enlightened the minds of the honest and honorable for more than 200 years? Yet its presence was tangible during both the friendly deals and the violent wars between our people. Those faithful can say, even if they don't fully understand it, that it will always be this way, for the secret is embraced only by some minds… even though many aspire to know it.

SPRING OF LIGHT

Chapter 1

Two Flemish Geniuses/
A Distant Find

In a small lab in the Faculty of Physics and Chemistry of Bruges University in Belgium, two extraordinary beings were in the middle of a whispered conversation, exchanging ideas. Apart from discussing the routine problems of the faculty, their conversation revolved around the news about a certain phenomenon found in a little town in Central America. According to them, there was a persistent light, variable in intensity, on the top of a hill that was a dormant volcano, which had erupted thousands of years before. These two phenomenal beings, as curious as any scientist and wisely humble, discussed the origin of that light. Their conversation didn't entertain the rushed theories of inexperienced minds or the fanatical baloney that ignorant people spread with stubbornness, as did the charlatan prophets that predicted the end of the world. They didn't waste their breath on the improbable or unprovable, such as miracles or alien invasions.

Their minds were strict, logical, worthy of distingui-shed faculty members who practiced disciplined research about heavy metals in their route from point A to point B, and the contrary forces that prevented their transfer. Each had already completed formulas that partially resolved the energy required by an element to counteract opposing forces—such as gravity, friction, or the very energy inhe-rent in the metal—and travel from one place to another as fast or as slow as the metal allowed. It had already been deduced and proved that a smaller quantity of a metal with a higher atomic number—a higher number of protons and neutrons in the nucleus and electrons around it, such as uranium—is capable of producing more radioactivity than large quantities of lighter elements, such as hydrocarbons. Their knowledge of these theories was one of the things that made them renowned experts in their field, earning them invitations into other research studies about dub-nium and meitnerium—very radioactive, synthetic metals with a short life span (minutes, even seconds) that makes them useless as stable or continuous energy sources.

The depth of their genius in the application of the quantum mechanics theory, which had already surpassed Bohr's, to analyze the characteristics of atoms and their way of dispersing energy as light had gained them recog-nition and honors from the university, the world, and their close circle of scientists who were trying to deal with the rising difficulties of humanity. Yet, their main interest was focused on solving the problems that gravity and friction caused for moving objects. "Why can't we all travel at the speed of light?" these geniuses asked themselves and each other.

They lived simple lives, avoiding the superfluous and the incongruent. Their undeniable genius allowed no frivolity, no unimaginative music, no repetitive music or undistinguishable music written by illiterates. They preferred silence to the trivialities favored by the youth without enthusiasm in searching the possible in what appears to be impossible. When they had time to read, they read only things related to their passion as scientists, for those were the masterworks in which the genius of mankind was expressed and palpable in its written beauty.

They both came from the fertile Kortemark fields and the settled Bruges suburbs; they could boast about no old lineage. As the centuries went by, disturbances, wars, and economic fluctuations forced the prized offspring out of the family nest, and many of them settled north of Michigan and Wisconsin, or even in the south of Canada, where communities spoke their language and practiced their customs. The main branch of their family tree still remain in Belgium. They were, truly, slaves to blood, for Dr. Marie Blomme Vandekandelaere was Otto Joseph Vandekandelaere's daughter, married to Hans Blomme Vandekandelaere, son to a distant relative of Otto's.

Hans was a diamond trader used to traveling frequently between Bruges and Antwerp. Father and daughter preferred to spend their weekends in their ancestral home in Kortemark, where family photos were kept, many of them memorializing relatives who had set sail for America and its promised riches.

In their backyard, a draft horse grazed, white, sturdy, and tame. Hernán, also in charge of keeping the house clean and ready for its owners, took care of the horse. Marie used to ride the horse whenever she wasn't drained of energy by lack of sleep and dedication to her profession. She was the director of the quantum mechanics division at the university. Her father was the vice-chancellor of the university and the director of the Faculty of Chemistry. He was fluent in four languages—Flemish, French, German, and English—and adamant that 90 percent of all science and its progress could be found documented in these languages.

One afternoon, after drinking a delicious and stimulating cup of coffee,[2] product of El Salvador, these two outstanding beings made the decision to request a three-month leave from the university to travel to Central

---

[2] Coffee is an invaluable gift from the Arabs to the world and is now recognized as a superfood for its incalculable benefits. But it's even better when enjoyed with a *semita de piña*, natives from El Salvador would add.

America and research the phenomenon known to them as the Light. Their wise instincts told them that the Light had its origin in something tangible and measurable that, in turn, had its origin in something very valuable, like a new element.

After a couple of weeks, having arranged for substitutes to cover them, the board approved their leaves, including their continued salaries and a $50,000 donation from the university's research fund to address eventual expenses. The Salvadoran embassy in Brussels, Belgium, took charge of additional preparations, including their welcome as honorary guests of the rectors from the three universities in El Salvador and arrangements for police protection during their commutes between the capital and the town, where they would live for three months, or on any other journeys they wished to make during their research.

The town's mayor was in charge of providing adequate accommodations for the two geniuses, and they managed to host them at a colonial house behind secure walls and conveniently placed one street away from the central park where the town's church was, two streets away from city hall.

The house was spacious. It had four bedrooms and four bathrooms, archways and interior columns, and three patios, the bigger of them behind the house where there was a little pool which was refreshing on hot days—in other words, most of the year. The other two were interior sunrooms, one of which formed the hub of the living room, dining room, and two bedrooms. It contained a flower bed filled with tropical flora and climbing vines that enhanced the view from the dining table.

To let in air and sunshine, in the middle of the side wall of the sunroom, there was a small glass window framed with mahogany and protected by a red-tile roof supported by ornamental-iron rafters. The sunroom was made even more attractive by ceramic tiles decorated with blue-framed white lilies embedded in a cement niche finished with porcelain. The tiles were made specially for the house by a *talavera* manufacturer in Puebla, México, which had been owned for more than a century by the same family who adhered to the traditional methods of crafting tiles first invented in Talavera de la Reina, Spain.

The third patio included a small garden in the front of the house; it contained palm trees and other tropical flora that framed the front entrance. The main entrance to the house was at the end of a little cement stairwell. The wood door was closed by an old lock that was opened by an enormous key as old as the lock it opened. The owners joked that the key could be used as a deadly weapon against any intruder.

The outside door was a pair of varnished mahogany doors decorated with a lion-shaped knocker. Inset into one of the doors was a little window with an ornamental metal frame; it could be opened and closed in order to see who was knocking at the door. The doors and entryway were protected by two roofs. One faced the street; the other, the garden. Both were made of red tile and supported by iron brackets on both sides of each door, front and back. Finally, the double doors were framed by a cement arch between two chiseled columns, one on each side, finished with the usual echinus, bell, and abacus. The voussoir had similar accents that created three rectangular and irregular figures. Lighting the doors was an old iron lantern hung from the roof that had been rewired to run on electricity.

As soon as the owners heard of the two scientists' intentions, they told the mayor that their house was ready; the scientists could enjoy their stay without worrying about paying rent. Additionally, the scientists were urged to swim in the pool as often as they wanted and to use the garden that was adjacent to four garages. It also offered fruit trees and a panoramic view of the town and its surrounding mountains.

The mayor would take care of feeding the scientists and the two security guards who would follow them everywhere. The guards were to sleep in the bedroom adjoining the garages and use the exterior bathroom with its own latrine, shower, and sink in which to wash clothes and utensils. The homeowners' guard would take care of the cleaning. With the university's financial assistance, the two geniuses would be able to afford a private cook and laundress.

All the accommodations and financial assistance produced a sense of well-being in the scientists, and they became more enthusiastic about the work they came to do. Having been seduced by the news of this so-called Light. They wanted to solve the mystery of its origin.

With his usual excitement, Otto had found an app to "learn Spanish in four weeks," so as often as he could, he studied common phrases that would allow him to communicate with the locals of that strange country to which he would donate his scientific genius, which would prove to be an unpredictable and formidable gift to the locals.

Father and daughter left Belgium as nervous and excited as children, thinking about all the new people and cultures they would encounter, things they had never imagined. They boarded the plane with an enthusiasm unfamiliar to their intellectual lives. They took each other's hand and, unable to stop smiling, found their seats in the first-class wing of the plane.

The scientists endured the long, tiring trip by taking multiple naps in their comfortable seats and reading short magazine articles about El Salvador. Once they began getting close to their destination, through their windows appeared a beautiful panoramic view of Central America with its impressive greenery and little towns isolated by never-ending mountains and uncountable hills; it was a beautiful region in which a network of streets meandered, weaving the towns of legend and history. The row of magnificent volcanoes appeared as if it were the carved spinal cord of a giant who supported this incredible chunk of the world.

As they approached the airport in San Salvador, the scientists took turns in the window seat so no one would miss the changing view. Suddenly, the crater of a volcano appeared and, at the foot of it, the capital city. There followed the coastline with multicolored plains cut into parcels by the different crops being grown, and then came the beaches of the Pacific Ocean with reddish sand that had been mixed with many millennia's ashes left by the volcanoes. "Painfully beautiful" had once been the description of a US volunteer on a medical mission to provide aid to homeless people in El Salvador.

Pulling large suitcases, the scientists proceeded through Immigrations and left behind the air-conditioned comfort of the airport. They were welcomed by a wave of suffocating heat and an entourage made up of representatives from the three universities, as well as the bodyguards and guide promised by El Salvador's embassy in Belgium. The sudden rise in temperature, normal for a tropical summer, took them by surprise.

At their hotel in the capital, they were amazed by the local cuisine that awaited them: crab, vegetables, cabbage soup, *arroz relleno*, corn with mayonnaise, *queso rallado* and coriander, a small ration of *semita de piña*, and lime sorbet. They were also offered Stella Artois, the Belgian beer, and they savored it with indescribable delight.

When they finished eating, a guitar trio appeared in the dining room. No introductions were needed; they started to play *huapangos y boleros*. The musicians surrounded the table and dedicated "Malagueña Salerosa," in beautiful falsetto, to Mary. She thanked them with the most beautiful smile imaginable; this was the first time she had been serenaded.

They retired to their respective bedrooms with a feeling of profound respect equal to the beauty and cordiality that they observed and received. They were anxious for dawn so they could head to the town that had excited their creative, curious minds.

The days after their arrival were spent installing a little lab in the warehouse after they emptied it, for it was full of trinkets they deemed unnecessary. They kept only a water tank, a boiler, and the washing machine. All the other trinkets were stored in another warehouse in the garden, next to the gardening tools and some piled-up plastic chairs used by the owners for special occasions like birthdays or Christmas. They also purchased a large blackboard and a box of chalk, white and red, with which to write and solve formulas as their work on the origin of the Light took flight.

Just like most geniuses of the world, they were modest and sparse in their way of dressing and weren't too fond of superfluous conversations that offered no new insights or knowledge. They didn't like rap music, for they found it monotonous and its verses lacking in inspiration. They preferred solitude and music by Handel and Brahms, especially the popular compositions like "Water Music," perhaps because the Dutch and the Flemish in particular tend to grow up in an atmosphere of order and calmness of spirit. This could explain why they didn't bring music by Chopin or Sibelius, but for unknown reasons did like Beethoven's sonatas for violin and piano and Beethoven's Fifth Symphony with its foreshadowing and universal message: the imperceptible desire to triumph over failure and the loneliness of death, the desire to find the unfindable, the truths not yet known by humanity. This symphony reflects, in its grand notes, the triumph of the spirit, man's will, and intelligence.

They were about to be so surprised by the town's patron-saint festivals and the musical groups, one on each of the six or seven street corners around the central park! Salsa and merengue were played for three or four days from six in the afternoon till midnight. If the scientists had any luck, their work there would be done before the festivals began.

One July morning, clear blue sky and no signs of rain, the two geniuses had breakfast at a wooden table and chairs. It was set up on the mansion's porch, which afforded a breathtaking view of the pool that was shaded by an evergreen bougainvillea in full bloom, red flowers cascading down to the pool's water, covering the whole surface. Next to the bougainvillea, built into the wall of the patio, there was a stone fountain decorated with four little ceramic tiles on the top. From the center of the fountain, a reddish tile canal stretched to the edge. Water sprang from the center and fell in the pool, like a little waterfall. The sound it made was lulling, perfect for calming the spirit, taking a nap, or going to bed during those dark, humid tropical nights.

Breakfast, as were all meals provided the geniuses, was prepared by the two best cooks in the town. One of them was Esther, who had a stand in the market and was known for her cleanliness. The other one, Reina, was hired by city hall to prepare food for them on weekends.

But the geniuses also wanted to know the customs of the town. They had already discovered the food stands and liked Chino Morataya and Chino's Pizza. They tried *tacos*, *pupusas*, and *banano* smoothies.

Today they were having fried eggs with green beans, *queso duro* with *tortillas*, black beans with cream, and pan dulce with their black coffee. This last one was known as the *veinte minutos*, for people said that one couldn't resist its diuretic effects for more than twenty minutes.

After breakfast, they made their way to the ravine and then to the top of the extinct volcano, the place where the Light was. They hired two workers to help them carry their equipment so the security guards could be free and alert should anything occur. They reached the María del Pilar Bridge and took pictures of women washing their clothes in the old *pilas*. Those workers gave them directions for the group's thousand-meter climb.

On their way up, father and daughter stopped every once in a while to take pictures of the colorful birds that flew through the branches of the wild fig trees. The birds' plumage was extraordinary and never before seen in Northern Europe; it imprinted itself on the souls of the geniuses. They were most impressed by the turquoise-browed motmot, *torogoz*, its iridescent colors and long tail of two feathers like wires that ended at the tip of the tail in fluffy green colors. One of their guides explained that that beautiful winged creature was the national bird. The geniuses used their cameras to take many zoomed pictures of that bird they could never have imagined and were grateful for having seen it in real life.

They walked past flowering coffee trees, little banana plantations, and passion-fruit trees, tall mango trees laden with fruit varying in shape, size, color, and flavor. Over a fence of one of the small farms, they saw the branches of a strange tree with smooth bark, little foliage, and small plump and long fruits. These green, yellow, and red fruits were sweet, and they delighted the workers and the guards.

The geniuses were surprised that everyone also ate the tender leaves of the tree. The geniuses didn't dare eat any, although the townsfolk offered them some; they were afraid of getting sick by eating things they weren't accustomed to. The guides explained that the name of that tree was *jocote*, or wild plum, and it loaned its name to the town in the Maya Lenka language, which meant *río de los jocotes*. Both geniuses already felt a kind of affection for the town, not only because of the authentic kindness of their welcome, but also because they'd heard that the owner of the house they were staying in was also Flemish and now resided in Tampa, Florida.

As they climbed the paths of the Chagüite River, the landscape changed. The Chagüite starts from the top of the mountain and runs down, forming little waterfalls and pools. In a pool fed by one of the small waterfalls, they saw a group of children and teenagers who were being watched by a couple of adults. The youngsters stood beneath the waterfall and dived into the pool, laughing and shouting, bringing joy to the hot morning. As expected, the geniuses took pictures of the group.

Later, though the crater was still far away, volcanic rock began to appear. Some of the rocks had *pilas* carved into them and were used for washing clothes and bathing. The water gradually changed temperature; it started to warm and got hotter as they climbed. A few meters ahead, they also noticed the mud of the riverbanks had changed color. The workers explained it was gypsum. They were approaching the area known as *La Viejona*.

The geniuses took samples of the colorful mud, using little plastic tubes they purposefully had brought. They looked at each other when they noticed a giant rock in the center of the river; it was different than the rest of the volcanic rock. This one was made up of reddish and dark-green veins that crossed its smooth face vertically. It also had shiny black veins that ringed it horizontally. The rest was just like every other rock in the area: opaque black surface, no noteworthy attributes.

They took pictures of the rock and continued climbing the hill, searching for the crater. It was covered by small trees and millennia's growth of weeds and mold that had been deposited by time. The geniuses discussed it and concluded they would search for other rocks like the one in the river. They opened their bags and took out little chisels and hammers, plus plastic tubes for samples, and began their search. With their feet and little shovels, they scratched the black soil that covered the crater, rested for a few moments, and continued with their search in other areas.

After a while, below the root of an *amate* tree, they noticed a protuberance of something that seemed enormous but was almost completely sunk into the earth. It was a smooth red rock crisscrossed by green veins. They cleaned the mold and the weeds from the surface and understood the enormity of the task and the impossibility of uncovering it with their small shovels. It seemed the rock almost filled the crater.

Hammer and chisel in hand, they took samples of the rock from various spots on its surface, including the veins. Though they dug beneath the soil almost a meter, they found no black rings, but did find the hairy black caterpillars common to environments in which the amate trees are found.

They had a small discussion and decided that they'd found something previously unseen by others, maybe singular, and that it would be better to keep it a secret until they analyzed the samples together.

They headed back to the town, and as they approached the rock in the river, Otto took off his shoes and socks, rolled up his pants, and, armed with hammer and chisel, got into the river and waded to the rock. He carved out little pieces of it, including samples from the rings.

The rest of the climb down was uneventful. After eating chicken soup and a plate of stuffed *güisquil*, with tortillas and orangeade, all prepared by Reina, they took a quick shower and sat talking in the rocking chairs on the patio. They were excited and smiling, rubbing their hands together like children.

Marie was the first one to affirm, "We will need potassium-40 to get an idea of the age of the rock. To get it, we must go back to Belgium. I would rather not go to the United States to do those analyses."

Dr. Otto completely agreed but suggested doing the preliminary analysis in the small makeshift lab of the house.

They both smiled at the prospect. They knew that the advanced research needed to determine atomic mass using a spectrometer would be impossible in El Salvador. Still, they decided to do the rudimentary analysis there, starting by pulverizing the rocks to analyze those samples under a microscope.

So they locked the door to the lab, drew a black curtain over the windows, and sat to enthusiastically do their work. They used a mortar to crush the samples and then catalogued them. Some of the samples were dry; others, humid. Using deionized water and microfilters, they strained the dust. Using different filters and various sources of light, including ultraviolet, they methodically recorded their observations in their notebooks.

The mud samples showed nothing out of the ordinary when observed in dry or wet media and under different sources of illumination. But recordable findings began to materialize when they started to analyze samples of the rock in the humid media; they observed a birefringence in the green-vein samples and a slight luminescence in the red veins of the rock.

Their surprise was even greater when they examined the black veins of the river rock. When the samples were exposed to ultraviolet light, an intermittent light, varying in intensity, was emitted. Then, when mixed with either red or green samples, the light dimmed and became a constant white glow. As the geniuses changed the angle of the ultraviolet light, the glow remained constant but changed to yellow.

After a quick rest, they wrote complicated formulas on the blackboard. After revising them, they decided to rest their minds, leaving the necessary corrections for the next day, when their mind would be clearer after a night's rest.

They dined in silence on corn tamales with cream, black beans, and the essential orangeade. For dessert, they had a cup of hot chocolate with *pan dulce*. They didn't talk about their findings, but instead listened to a Beethoven sonata before going to sleep.

The next morning, after having a quick breakfast while listening to the calming sound of the water falling from the fountain into the pool, they reviewed the formulas on the board and were happy to know that both had arrived at the same conclusion. They could explain the light phenomenon using current physics and chemistry parameters, theoretical or nontheoretical. The mystery of the light would be solved with a simple horizontal formula, beginning by identifying the elements found at the ravine and assuming that the light emanated from those elements.

It was obvious that every step would require a proved methodology in which quantum mechanics would play a role, as would the effect of different sources of light: shortwave laser, ultraviolet, sunlight, etc.

What they wrote on the board—and agreed there would be no deviations from; every step would have a mathematical explanation—was this:

A. Element or metal x = inner/internal energy (electrons) = Watt/Kilowatt = Joules= Photon/Boson = La Luz

B. Element/metal x = high atomic mass = high # of isotopes (neutrons) = high fission (fusion?) = ↑ energy $(E=mc2)$ = La Luz

They immediately decided to gather more rock samples. Their first step was to determine the atomic weight, atomic number, and number of electrons (which are usually the ones that absorb and store energy) of the element they had found, element x. They had to go back to Belgium to perform these analyses.

Preparations for a second expedition to the ravine for the following day were made. This was reported to their guides and guards, for they wished to climb to the rock as soon as possible. They gathered their hammers, chisels, and now larger containers for samples, and rested on the rocking chairs, listening to the waterfall, for the remainder of the day.

Reina made lemonade, myrtle juice, and mango juice for their delight. They were curious about the myrtle tree; one of them grew in the neighboring garden, so after lunch, they climbed a little hill to reach the garden and took photographs. The caretaker opened the gate, and, sailing like children, they ran into the garden, which was full of pleasant surprises.

The garden had cobblestone paths that led to little corners, shadowed by tall tropical trees, with cement benches. The gazebo, made of stone and cement, and covered by an old reddish-tile roof, impressed them. They took several pictures and swung on a hammock that was set up for them inside the gazebo. In most of these pictures, they are smiling and making a peace sign with their fingers.

Wind produced music as it ran through metal tubes, a vibraphone, that hung in a corner of the gazebo. They took pictures of the town and the surrounding mountains; in some of them, they in the foreground. Then they walked to another part of the garden and found strange trees, at least for them, like *arrayán, cacao, níspero, mamey, limonero, naranjo, mandarino,* and *pomelo. Cocotero, mango, guayabo, aguacate,* and a field with never-ending flowers that attracted butterflies and hummingbirds.

In the corner of the garden stood a rectangular fountain framed by a hundred ceramic tiles affixed with white grout. Each tile had a strange last name engraved on it and different dates, starting from 1995 and ending in 2011. At its center, a giant tile, multicolored and decorated with arabesques, read "Fuente the los Voluntarios," Volunteers' Fountain. It was explained to them that the fountain was dedicated to the doctors, nurses, ophthalmologists, surgeons, dentists, pediatricians, and other volunteers, foreigners and *salvadoreños*, who had provided free medical and surgical care to the town and its neighboring villages from 1995 to 2011. Thanks to a New York philanthropist and his family, and the construction of a small but beautiful fully equipped and stocked hospital with surgical rooms, their mission was successful.

Each tile honored the personal efforts of a volunteer. Some of them seemed to be Indian, Italian, German, French, English, Spanish, Canadian, Mexican, Argentinian, Guatemalan, Pakistani, and Ethiopian, but most of all Salvadoran and American. Even a Belgian was memorialized by a tile bearing the name of the owner of the house in which the scientists were hosted.

They returned from the garden sweaty, which made Marie want to refresh herself in the pool. Otto didn't want to take a dip; instead, he took off his shoes and sat at the edge, his feet in the water, to stay cool. He was so comfortable that he declared, "When we come back to this town, I'll get in this pool!"

They leisurely dined, listened to Brahms, delighted in "Peer Gynt," and went to their respective beds, satisfied with their achievements in the town.

The next day, father and daughter began making the arrangements to return to Belgium, for the night before they had decided it was better to go back to Belgium with the samples than to make another trip to the ravine. They packed their instruments and the rocks they would analyze in anticipation of presenting their valuable findings to humanity.

After breakfast, they said goodbye to their guides and the caretaker and headed to the capital. Their bodyguards took them to a hotel in which they would wait for their flight back to Belgium the next day.

At the airport, they priority-checked their bags; they had first class seats that guaranteed them rest and a snack. They were making a stopover in New York.

They touched down in Brussels at ten in the morning, a day after leaving El Salvador. They were as tired as they looked. A minivan was waiting for them outside the airport, courtesy of Bruges University, to take them to their homes.

Coming home filled them with emotion, although they were tired; they hadn't slept from Brussels to Bruges. All they did was admire the panoramic view of their home country, and their souls were grateful for belonging to such a beautiful place.

In Bruges, they ate clams and potatoes and drank Rioja wine. In celebration, they each had a glass of Stella Artois, the pride of Belgium. Delighted, they went to their homes.

They slept for ten hours, under a shy sun that refused to come out, and awoke to a rainy European morning. They were back home!

* * *

Back in El Salvador, however, the town was in chaos. Curiosity had been awakened in the people the geniuses had interacted with, and those people had questions for the guides. When they found out the reason for the climb, they spread the news to whoever would listen. And so dozens of people, armed with hammers, stones, and nails, climbed the ravine and tore at the rock to get big and small pieces of stone.

The commotion caused by the invaders of the ravine concluded in quarrels, for everyone wanted to get their hands on the "best" piece of rock. They felt deceived and told themselves, "If those Europeans are finding value in these rocks, there's no way I'm not getting some." This was a matter of ignorance and greed that forced the mayor's office to build a wire fence around the ravine, which was monitored by two cops in a guardhouse. Only those with a special permit issued by the mayor's office could traverse the ravine.

As always, the greedy protested, but the mayor, wisely, paid no attention and ordered the ravine permanently watched until the geniuses' return. They had told him they would come back as soon as their research was completed and they had determined the rock's metal composition, its origin and properties.

The mess and damage in the ravine were the same as what was happening in the Volunteers' Fountain. It had endured, at the hands of ill-mannered people, the pilfering of stones and tiles, especially those with the names of the volunteers who had traveled from far-off countries to lend the town their knowledge, expertise, and professionalism, gifting the homeless with medicine, surgery, and ophthalmological attention, even to the point of excising tumors to restore both sight and health. And this—the stealing of the tiles on which their names were written—was how the ungrateful repaid them for fifteen years of selfless service.

The vandalism and stealing became so rampant that the owner of the garden was compelled to move the fountain to a spot that no outsiders, thieves, or vandals could reach. And so the fountain was lifted from its foundation of earth and rock by a bricklayer who was an artisan, Fais Perreira. He carefully numbered each piece and prepared for transport the 3,500-kilogram fountain. With the help of three men, each piece was wrapped in a thick blanket, to protect it from smashing, and then arranged in the bed of a truck in a way that ensured the pieces wouldn't bump against each other or the sides of the truck. Fais ordered the truck's driver to go slowly and avoid any bumps or holes that might jar and shatter the tiles.

When the pieces finally arrived at the fountain's new home, Fais reassembled it, piece by piece, tile by tile. For reference and to resolve any puzzlement along the way, he used photographs of the original to ensure that it was restored perfectly. This took Fais two months, working nonstop ten to twelve hours a day, seven days a week. He accepted no advice, no pleas for rest until the fountain was complete and looked as it used to.

As with everything Fais did, the excavation, transportation, and reassembly of the Volunteers' Fountain was a testament to the love Fais, the genius artisanal bricklayer, had for his work. So even though he wasn't a volunteer for the medical missions, his name was memorialized on one of the tiles in a special spot on the fountain's wall.

* * *

Awakened from their long, restful sleep, the geniuses contemplated the dark, rainy Bruges morning. Unintentionally, their spirits hearkened back to the hot, fresh tropical days, and they missed and loved that tiny Central American town even more.

Breakfast was short—Belgian waffles covered in raspberry syrup, a hard-boiled egg with salt and mustard (this they learned about in El Salvador); to finish, Salvadoran coffee and *semita de piña*, which they had brought back in their suitcases. Their longing grew for that town that had gifted them with such happy, productive days.

After breakfast, father and daughter prepared for their meeting with the university's executive board to present their findings and plan their next steps. They assembled folders, notes, photographs of their formula-filled blackboard, and samples of the rock.

The meeting was friendly and playful, for everyone tried to greet each other using bad Spanish. Otto, keeping the joke going—with a large grin, which was weird for him—even dared to correct the others. He believed himself "almost an expert in the language," for, as he put it, "What good is there in living in a country for three weeks and not learning anything from its people?" He explained that, in El Salvador, almost every question ended with the word *"pues"* as a way of stressing the question—for example, *"Te divertiste, pues?"*[3] *"Y cuántos años tenés, pues?"*[4] *"Y ya te casaste, pues?"*[5] And so on.

---

[3] Did you have fun, then?

[4] So how old are you, then?

[5] You married yet, then?

As Otto and Marie talked about their findings, there was dead silence in the boardroom of Bruges University, for the executive board was composed of scientists like Otto and Marie; their minds were always open and receptive to the previously unknown. New knowledge stimulated their thinking and allowed them to apply logic to finding novel, innovative solutions.

There came a moment when one of those scientists voiced the logical question, "What if the rock was part of Theia? What if it is now exposed because a volcanic eruption brought it to the surface?"

The board looked at him with approving smiles, perhaps because he had asked the question that was on everybody's mind even though no one else had dared voice it.

Before the meeting ended, they agreed on a budget for the completion of the research on the strange rock that Otto and Marie had found. Their aim was to identify its elements and determine if they had practical applications for mankind.

* * *

Thea is a little planet that crashed into Earth during its infancy. The impact shattered both planets into a million pieces. One of those pieces became our Moon. Earth was ruptured by the impact, its surface divided into enormous tectonic plates.

Between these plates, massive cracks formed; we now call these cracks "faults." The longest is the San Andreas Fault, extending from Alaska to the South Pole. Tectonic plates frequently collide, producing and releasing an unfathomable quantity of energy that is responsible for geological events like tsunamis and earthquakes. Volcanoes and mountain ranges form along these faults. When one mass pushes with great force against another, the ground squeezes upwards, forming mountain ranges of great altitudes. When the impact is light, even mere scrapes, the buildup of energy is dissipated through smaller, sometimes imperceptible, tremors.

In Central America, a thousand tremors are recorded monthly. The same thing happens in Alaska and along the entire coast of the Pacific Ocean in South America. Central America is, therefore, a trembling paradise.

Theia brought great benefits to our planet. It not only caused an era of water, which eventually made life possible on Earth, but it is also responsible for bringing to Earth, as part of its mass, most of the metals known today, and perhaps even those yet unknown. The force of Theia's collision changed the Earth's rotation on its axis and its orbit around the sun, which brought us our changing seasons.

The little planet became part of our Earth, making the center of our planet denser and heavier than its surface. It is also possible that volcanic eruptions, using fumaroles that originate at the center of the Earth, have been pushing to the surface Theia's elements, including the one being studied by our two Belgian geniuses.

Great astrophysicists postulate that the impact between Earth and Theia occurred five billion years ago. The immensely high temperatures that were reached during the impact would've vaporized any solid matter and blended together much of the Earth's and Theia's metals. As time went by, most of the liquid metals returned to their solid state, were discovered by man, and eventually classified using the periodic table.

The metals that spark the interest of our two geniuses are uranium and plutonium, for the relative ease with which technicians and specialists can manipulate these metals to produce a vast amounts of energy with small amounts of those two metals. As they wrote Einstein's formula, $E=mc^2$, on their blackboard, it occurred to them that this quality could also exist in the metal they had found in the ravine.

* * *

In the board meeting, the first agreed-upon step was to identify and date the metal using the thermal ionization mass spectrometer of the university and the potassium-40 technique Marie had suggested. Parallel studies were going to be conducted, including gathering basic information about the metal, atomic number, atomic mass, etc., just to begin deducing where it would fit on the periodic table; that would help determine its potential for producing energy.

The studies were extensive. Each time new information was found, similar scientific methods corroborated it. In subsequent meetings of the executive board, which were always attended by our two geniuses, the valuable, highly scientific progress was discussed, such as atomic number, atomic weight, radiometric dating of the rock according to the mass spectrometer that used thermal ionization, results of optical emission spectroscopy in inductively coupled plasma, yoctograms of a proton by nanotechnology, using carbon nanotubes to measure the vibration frequency of the metal, and other descriptive terminology of modern techniques used to identify, as fully as possible, the nature of a metal.

Names of several theories and chemical, physical, and quantum laws were also thrown around. These would eventually form the basis of the metal's presentation to the scientific world. Amongst the names mentioned were Einstein, Planck, Bohr, Newton, Oppenheimer, Schrödinger, Heisenberg, von Braun, etc.

From all the different labs in charge of analyzing the samples, there came pleasant surprises. One of them was that the radiometric dating proved that the rock's age dated back to the time of the Earth's collision with Theia, meaning that the rock was approximately four billion years old. Doctor Emil VanDerKluge smiled when he heard the news; he had been the one to suggest that the rock's origin could've been Theia. Simple as that. Emil received the congratulations of his colleagues who hoped that the subsequent news about the metal would also be favorable.

And so, what Marie and Otto had been waiting for finally came. The mass spectrometer analysis indicated that the metal in the rock was a post-uranium with a gigantic atomic weight. Up to that point, it was predicted that the rock's atomic number would exceed 120, which meant that the metal would rank outside of today's periodic table.

Even outside the artificially created heavy metals. These are created by experts using the neutron-bombardment method, which produces isotopes that convey different qualities to the bombarded metal, thus resulting in an artificial metal mostly useless to humanity.

Yet, this time, the metal in question existed in nature. The next step was to identify it and study its possibilities as a fissionable energy source—an everlasting source of energy capable of rescuing humanity from its dependence on nonrenewable energy sources that would eventually be depleted.

Otto and Marie had foreseen this outcome from the beginning as they studied the rock in a rudimentary makeshift laboratory in the old storeroom of an old house somewhere in El Salvador, armed only with one microscope, a light, a board, colored chalk, and a notebook. When they exposed the black-ring samples taken from the rock to ultraviolet light, they emitted a white shimmer. This observation caused them to look at each other with smiles of satisfaction, for they had almost certainly guessed at what the black rings of the rock represented. Their minds had immediately traveled to the laws of electromagnetism and all its real-life applications. So they had immediately written the simple deduction on their blackboard, something already proved by some of humanity's geniuses (Faraday, Maxwell, Planck, Einstein, etc.). It could be reduced to the following: energy = quanta.[6]

ENERGY = QUANTA = LIGHT = VISIBLE
COLOR IN THE SPECTRUM AND
REFLECTED BY OBJECTS

SPECTRUM = SEVEN BASIC COLORS,
SUMMARIZED IN WHITE

---

[6]An indivisible particle of an atom that absorbs, keeps, and releases energy.

AND ABSORBED IN BLACK

ULTRAVIOLET = LIGHT THAT CAN FREE
AND DISPERSE THE SEVEN COLORS
ABSORBED IN BLACK

BLACK RINGS OF THE ROCK = MAIN
SOURCE OF ENERGY EMANATING
FROM THE ROCK
GREEN VEIN = INTERMEDIATE
SOURCE OF ENERGY

RED VEIN = TINY
SOURCE OF ENERGY

Even if seemingly simple, these observations were based in reality, on the laws of physics, chemistry, and quantum mechanics, in which both were experts, thanks to their lives' dedication to science. And so, even simple observations—such as those about the refraction of the light on the metal, which were noticed when the rock was studied under both humid and dry conditions—had fundamental reasoning behind them: deionized water, which they used to study the samples, was identical to the vapor that emanated from ravine; both forms of water (vapor or liquid) were free from the pollution of elements that were not found in water. That was how they reproduced in a warehouse laboratory the variables of what nature did every day at the top of a ravine—the temperature of the volcanic subsoil, the ultraviolet light of the sun, and a metal unknown until then. This was the how the Light was produced.

Progress on the research was slow but sure, for a rigorous scientist knows that rushing to get to the end, sooner or later, brings failure. Slowly, it was determined that the new metal wasn't amongst those already predicted to be missing from the periodic table. It was also determined that the metal had a high percentage of unstable isotopes capable of releasing energy or radioactivity. Uranium possesses less than 1 percent of these isotopes, yet that small percentage is capable of producing and releasing immense quantities of energy essential to human life and the movement of immense machines. However, man has also been known to use this energy to create lethal weapons, like bombs, capable of condemning us to a universal catastrophe beyond fixing, no way out.

The percentage of radioactive isotopes in the new metal seemed to be higher than in uranium. It was initially calculated to be between 3.7 and 4.1 percent of its total mass.

The executive board burst with joy when they found out. Hugs for Otto and Marie for their great discovery were well deserved, for the board recognized their honesty and humility, and the diligence with which their scientific life had flowed.

That very day, Doctor Marie Blomme Vandekandelaere proposed the new metal be named after that region in El Salvador, to bring honor to their people. Lenkanium was the name she suggested, which was accepted—no discussion needed. Again, the humility of soul in both of the Belgian geniuses shone with a most eloquent splendor; that is what illuminates, separates, and elevates greatness. Inside Otto and Marie, you'd find no arrogance, no demands for recognition. They could've easily proposed another name, something that referenced their country, their last names, or their first names, just as many of the discoverers of other metals tended to demand. But, no, the horizon of their minds was wider, nobler; they weren't looking for fame or prestige.

Again, Marie, Otto, and the executive board celebrated, not with champagne, but with bottles of Stella Artois, the queen brew of Belgium.

That magnificent day, the members of the board promised each other that the presentation of the information to the government of El Salvador regarding the discovery of the new metal would be led personally by Otto and Marie as soon as possible. The ravine needed to be closed to the public, for it was impossible to know for sure how much of the surface the whole rock took. The energy experts in Belgium would be informed too, but later, after eliminating the names of anyone allegedly tied to suspicious activity.

They outlined a pact between El Salvador and the energy companies in Belgium that would later mine the metal. And they formulated a contract that forever and until the end of time prohibited the sale of even the barest amount of the metal to governments that would exploit its radioactive qualities for the production of weapons. The metal would have to be used to better lives, never to bring death and tragedy to any place on our beautiful planet.

Plans were made, documents were written, and Otto and Marie's return to El Salvador was all set. It would all be done with discretion; there would be no press conference to forewarn the country. Access to the ravine would be banned, effective immediately, by the government of El Salvador; included in the ban were all properties around the ravine, from María del Pilar Bridge to the top of the mountain and everything around it. And then, for good measure, they extended the banned area a few more meters.

El Salvador's government would exercise their right of eminent domain to fund and buy, at a fair price, all the properties identified by the scientists and the board in order to maintain a secure perimeter around the ravine. Guardhouses would also be installed in the four cardinal points, at the foot of the mountain, for protection against intruders.

The discovery was slowly creating an aura of happy anticipation, the extent of which was yet to be imagined. Everyone was waiting to find out the physical, verifiable qualities of the metal and how much of it could be extracted from the ravine.

The executive board hired expert Belgian and Dutch geologists to accompany Otto and Marie on a "geological mission to a region in El Salvador." No more details were given to the geologists, for none of them were members of the executive board, and they feared news of the discovery would leak.

Days passed, and the last details about the metal were still missing. What was the exact number of protons and neutrons in the nucleus? How many electron orbits could the metal possess? And, most importantly, how many suborbitals in the first and second energy levels did the metal have? The answer to this last question depended in great part on its potential as a trustworthy energy source. Once all these questions were answered, the research on the valence of the metal and the tridimensional image of its molecules would be conducted as accurately as possible.

But that this metal was extraordinary was already known; that is why they were already discussing how to mine it and what its practical applications would be. That's why the protection of the ravine and keeping it out of foreign hands was essential. El Salvador was a poor country, but now it had the potential to enter an unimaginable era of prosperity.

Yet greed has no limits, knows no boundaries, and its arrival must be stopped at all costs; all doors must be closed to the sly who wished to bilk all possible gains from the rock, no matter the cost. The country was in need of the humility, nobility, and perseverance of the Belgian geniuses.

Emil VanDerKluge was the group's cowboy, known for his joviality and genius. He was invited on the El Salvador trip, accompanying Otto, Marie, and the geologists. Emil grew three inches and could no longer fit in his seat as he burst with pride when he received the invitation. He got up from his seat and embraced Otto and Marie, so grateful for their trust. The executive board was happy to have Emil as part of the project.

When the results from the potassium-40 analysis of the rock arrived, the scientists in the executive board joked again. The analysis suggested that the rock was approximately 3,600 million years old. It was Emil who made the board burst into laughter when, with the stone-cold delivery sometimes necessary to dissolve the tension in the geniuses' demeanor, he declared, "We won't start a fight in the name of a few million years, *pues*!" He intentionally used the Salvadoran word, which made the board laugh even more.

NOTES: At first glance, we can tell the last names of these geniuses belong to prominent North European lineages, from which we can infer that, with the passing of time, throughout the years and centuries, genetic evolution in these families has produced cerebrums predisposed to thinking outside the box and recognizing the symbolism in music and numbers (science).

Chapter 2

In Belgium / Return to El Salvador

No one could've guessed at the hidden beauty Marie's appearance disguised. She wore an enormous pair of tortoiseshell glasses behind which she had hazelnut-colored eyes. Her hair was reddish-brown and thick; she always wore it in a ponytail. Her face knew no makeup, and yet her skin and rosy cheeks spoke of a healthy life of methodical reasoning far away from stupid vices. She had an oval, symmetrical face with a sharp nose that was a bit aquiline, evidence of her Flemish heritage and true to the saying, "There are no upturned noses in Flanders."

She was five feet, four inches tall, which was average for a Belgian woman. In a gym close to her home, she exercised three times a week, and she followed a strict diet that did not allow epicurean excesses, as evidenced by the ideal weight she maintained, 120 pounds.

At thirty-three years of age, she hid her athletic frame under oversized shirts, awful cargo pants made of thick material, the pockets stuffed with her notepads, pencils, phone, money, wallet, cards, IDs, family photos, bills, and a collection of little folded pieces of paper on which she'd scribbled scientific notes. Eventually, these notes would find their way to a wooden box inside one of her desk's drawers. That box was filled with the proof of her genius and the flashes of brilliance her brain dictated that she jot down lest her ideas be forgotten. That's the way of genius: exotic and unpredictable.

Marie carried an enormous gray-leather messenger bag that was always filled with books. It had long leather shoulder straps and hung down to her knees as she walked with purpose. She carried herself as someone who was determined and focused on a goal, wasting no time on enjoying her surroundings or other small worries like the end of the world, for example.

The weekend before going back to El Salvador, Otto, Marie, and Hans traveled to Kortemark in hopes of clearing their minds and apprising Hernán of their planned absence. They spent two days relaxing, which helped them forget about daily worries.

That Sunday afternoon, they returned to Bruges, all smiles, having chitchatted the entire way. The preparations for the Bruges University group's return to El Salvador were as complete as possible. Various rounds of revisions were made to the equipment list and its functionality. It was going to be used, if possible, to calculate the total surface of the rock, as well as its overall height, including the portion buried deep in the ravine. They would be using the most modern and sophisticated instruments available at the time. Even though some of the equipment performed similar functions, even identical ones, they would use the equipment from several manufacturers for verification of the data to avoid later criticism about certain pieces of equipment being less reliable than others. In addition to instruments to help classify the origin of the rock, they took two seismographs, two ground-penetrating radars, a Vernier micrometer, a measuring tool for mapping or topographic surveying of the terrain around the crater.

The Salvadoran embassy in Brussels was in charge of organizing interviews for the members of the group, excluding the geologists, with representatives from El Salvador's government. The embassy also made arrangements to ensure that the group's arrival in the country was as discreet as possible: they would circumvent usual Immigrations processing and be welcomed in a VIP room.

* * *

Departure day finally arrived. Joseph, Marie, and the geologists traveled calmly, pensively, inside the bus that took them from Bruges to Brussels International Airport. Emil was the only one who could not stay in his seat due to the excitement that his smile and constant questions made evident. His optimism and loquacity slowly rubbed off on his fellow travelers.

By the time they were almost at the airport, everybody was singing as well as they could, some stutteringly, the famous *"Cielito Lindo,"* which Emil had searched for on the internet and copied down on sheets he passed out to the travelers. As expected, the stolid Dutch geologists couldn't wholeheartedly commit to such secular frivolity; they were content to only hum along. Nevertheless, it brought everyone a moment of happiness.

After a twelve-hour trip, which included a two-hour layover in Mexico City, they landed in San Salvador at three in the afternoon on a cloudy day at the end of October. Central America's hurricane season was waning, and a dry, temperate summer was expected to start in November in the high regions of the isthmus.

Yet, as always, the last roar of winter was making itself known with a first-class downpour that made the travelers nervous. They had already cleared Immigrations and Customs when they were greeted by directors of the three great universities in San Salvador, as well as by the minister of the interior and his entourage.

Then our travelers boarded a comfortable bus that would take them to their hotel; it was followed by the six sedans it took to transport the welcome committee. That was when, as they drove through the little mountains on the way to San Salvador, the downpour morphed into a ferocious gale storm.

The drivers quickly looked for a place to take cover. They chose a nearby hamlet to wait out the storm, for the rain was, in all seriousness, a thick curtain of water that blocked all visibility.

Patiently and in spite of their weariness after the long trip, Flemish and Dutch waited for an hour. When the storm finally subsided, it was full dark outside, but they continued their trip nonetheless. These types of storms, very common during Central American winters, were a surprise for the travelers; their countries did not experience weather extremes of this type, especially such quick changes—nature's growling fury followed by a smiling calm.

When they finally arrived at the hotel, they were completely exhausted. They had a *gallina* and vegetable soup for dinner, accompanied by French bread, *queso duro*, Rioja wine, and apple pie with lime ice cream for dessert. After dinner, they rushed to their rooms and slept for the ten hours their tired bodies needed to recover.

The next day, at nine o clock in the morning, all the travelers were up for breakfast, gathered and seated around a big table set for them in the ample dining room of the hotel, which also boasted a breathtaking view of the enormous volcano. The area around the volcano was slowly succumbing to new construction: buildings, houses, and apartment buildings that extended right up to the foot of the volcano.

The geologists couldn't hide their reactions; they were awestruck by the beauty around them, which was unique and strange to them. They quietly took it all in, filling their souls with the roaring life of the tropics. With a big smile on their faces, they tapped each other on the shoulder as a sign of approval; they had made the right decision in coming with the Flemish to such beautiful country.

The morning dawned bright and fresh, thanks to the previous day's rain. The group was anxious to begin the trip towards the town that was their goal, so at ten in the morning, they boarded their bus, which was driven by the same driver as the night before. Stomachs full, they exchanged greetings and got ready for a two-hour trip, 130 kilometers.

Comfortable in their seats, they began speaking in English, even though Otto and Marie were fluent in Dutch, for it resembled their native language. During the ride, the newbies, especially Emil and the Dutch, admired the beauty of the natural scenery the winter storms provided. Green was the predominant color, bright and varied, and there were fruits that would soon be sold in the little *champas*, made either of sticks or metal sheets, that bordered the road ahead. They were also surprised by the obvious poverty of the farmers, whose houses were built on both sides of the road.

Again, it was Emil who, in a whisper, started to sing "Cielito Lindo," and this time it was Joseph who, thanks to his efforts to learn Spanish, accompanied Emil's whispered hums. Joseph, an extremely intelligent man whose brain was an insatiable sponge that absorbed anything new, had actually learned Spanish and some regional dialects of El Salvador.

Joseph then asked, imitating the *Guanaco* accent, "*Y qué, no te sabés otra canción vos, pues?*"[7]

The driver burst out laughing, as did the other passengers.

The trip went on without incident. The passengers even stopped to take some pictures of the Jiboa Valley and, ahead, the Lempa River that was full and, thanks to the copious rain, almost overflowing. The river's immensity made the travelers think about the great rivers of Europe on which they had sailed and whiled away the hours.

At noon, they reached the town. The old colonial house was, as it had been for Joseph and Marie, ready to house them. Reina had lunch already prepared for them:

---

[7] "Don't you know another song, then?"

camarones al ajillo, arroz relleno, parmesan cheese, corn *tortillas,* mango and myrtle juice, and orangeade. For dinner, she had prepared, ready for them in the fridge, spaghetti and meatballs in *tomate, pimiento y pepita de calabaza sauce,* and steamed vegetables, for she was warned to steam all vegetables to prevent intestinal infections in the foreigners. Reina would be back in the afternoon to heat the *viandas*[8] and serve them. She wanted their first day in town to go as swiftly and smoothly as possible.

Each guest was shown to one of the four bedrooms in the house. A few minutes later, Emil was spotted in his bathing suit and rubber flip-flops, carrying a towel; he was ready to dive into the pool.

When he did, he screamed surprisedly, "The water's freezing!" He proceeded to splash around and put his head under the waterfall.

Envy did its work, and the Dutch hurried to catch up. As they dove into the water, they were pleading with Emil to stop singing "Cielito Lindo."

The charm of that old house, with its archways and columns, filled everyone with an unexpected sense of peace. All afternoon, they spent unpacking their suitcases and putting the equipment in order, ready to start.

---

[8] Sustenance.

The mayor's office sent four policemen to act as guides and bodyguards. They presented their IDs to the travelers and offered their help in showing them around the town. When they were ready to climb the ravine, the policemen would accompany them.

After dinner that afternoon, they climbed to the neighboring garden and went to the gazebo at the overlook. While the rest meandered along the paths and into the corners of the beautiful garden, Marie settled in a hammock that the guard had set between two pillars.

They returned to the house when it was already dark, and Marie insisted on listening to her music, so they all delighted in a Beethoven sonata before retiring.

They woke early the next morning. Esther prepared fried eggs with *salsa ranchera*, black refried beans with cream, *tamales de elote*, *queso duro-blando*, corn *tortillas*, orange juice, and medium-elevation black coffee, which was in season and the first crop of November. It was impossible to get five-thousand-feet-elevation coffee, for that coffee ripens slower and is harvested from December to January. It is known for its smoothness and chocolate aftertaste.

When they arrived, the patronal festivals had already ended, but there remained some merchants who sold typical candies and *chucherías.*[9] The vendors were already packing up their *puestos*[10] and *tiliches*[11] to move to other towns, other patronal festivals. Yet the Europeans were able to buy some typical candies that caught their attention, such as grapefruit candy with a cherry in the middle, marzipans, mini *dulces de tapa* covered in *tuza de maíz*, delicious tamarind candies, *canillas de dulce de leche, cocadas,* and anything else that was left for sale that they wanted to taste. They also saved some to take back to Belgium and Holland to share with family and friends.

The policemen arrived early and were already waiting on the street for the Europeans to finish breakfast so they could climb up the ravine together. Recent October rains and winds, foretelling the arrival of a tropical summer, freshened the atmosphere and invigorated the spirit. Four lads had been hired to help carry the equipment.

On its way to the ravine, the party impressed the townsfolk who passed by them, already running errands in the market or relaxing on the benches of the park. Fifteen members made up the party; they brought to mind images of old films about safaris, for the five Europeans wore identical khaki clothing, and the same color hats. The

---

[9] Junk food.

[10] Stands.

[11] Things.

lads carrying the equipment followed in single file. Marie carried a parasol. The six policemen watched their backs.

The only thing missing to complete the image was one of the Europeans lighting a pipe and the distant scream of Tarzan letting Jane and Chita know that he was on his way back home, swinging on vines and with a killer hunger, for he had just killed a lion and vanquished an entire European army that was running around bothering people. This would all be communicated in the cryptic language of the great monkeys, which Tarzan had learned as a baby. "UMBAWE! KWANGANDA! TARZÁN! UMBAWE! ZULUANDA! WANDANGA!" This famous scream would pierce the jungle and desert just to communicate to Jane that *"Ahí te dejé madurando unos guineos majonchos pa' la Chita y te traigo una piel de cocodrilo pa' que te hagás unas carteras y le des una grande al jefe de los Zulú y otra más chiquita pa' la mujer del jefe de los Ban Dar."*[12] The treacherous dwarfs had always been *cheros*[13] of Tarzan. While Jane, always sharp with business deals and an expert in the dialect of the great monkeys, listened as she tended to her academy and instructed European tourists.

---

[12] I left some *majoncho* bananas ripening for you, and I'm bringing a crocodile's skin so you can craft a purse, a big one, for the chief of the Zulú, and a little one for the Ban Dar's chieftess.

[13] Buddies.

Several kids, curious, approached the party to say hi and ask the Europeans in broken English, *"Jaguar[14] yu?"*

To which, the nice travelers replied with sincere smiles that expressed how pleased they were to be in this strange, somewhat primitive country and to be greeted and welcomed with such kindness and joy. They felt sure they were on the right path towards changing the world; millions of inhabitants were going to benefit from the metal they'd found in that country, a country that now felt like home to them.

The climb to the ravine was slow and uneventful. The rains had caused the river to swell and the paths to become slippery. Swimmers and women washing clothes could still be seen in the little streams or on the riverbanks. These people were banned from climbing the ravine; a metal fence barred the way to all except those carrying a special permit from the mayor's office.

The fence started at approximately 250 meters from the river's entry into the gorge that divides the town in two. Two guardhouses, one on each side of the river, protected the ravine from intruders who might disturb the rock or its surroundings. The vigilance was constant, with guards rotating on twelve-hour shifts.

---

[14] Literally, "jaguar," the feline, which in Spanish is an homonym for "how are."

But the initial objections of the townsfolk about being denied access to the ravine gradually died down as reason won them over. It was obvious to most of them that what the ravine hid was going to be beneficial for the town.

The policemen who accompanied the Europeans saluted toward the guardhouse, and the guards within opened a little gate in the fence so the party could access the ravine.

Words of admiration were muttered by Emil, the Dutch soon joining him, as they started to notice the different types of birds that inhabited the mountain. Especially when they saw the beautiful *torogoz,* a bird that they could never have even imagined.

Emil was the first one to speak. "We will have to protect the habitat of these beautiful birds and make them an essential part of our reports."

They all agreed with Emil's wise idea, for this meant that any decision in choosing a mining company would be based on the willingness of the company to commit to never inflicting irreparable damage on the area in which those beautiful winged creatures lived and grew.

The most beautiful of the birds was the *torogoz,* a rival of the *quetzales* that don't sing but chirp. The *torogoz* in the mountains of El Salvador act as a balm that heals the wounds of the soul; no one should be allowed to touch them, hurt them, or hamper their freedom. When the *torogoz* finally sings, the murmurs of the jungle cease, and all living things stand still and listen. Its song, almost a cry, is the whisper that lulls the soul of the homeland; it is sadness's hymn for a race ever hunted. It prompts the question for fate: "Until when?"

As Emil delighted in the exquisite beauty of the bird, his consciousness, that of a noble man, was filled with the need to protect the habitat of such a splendid creature—solitary in its travels through the thick woods; docile but not tame; free on its mountain, as it should be.

El Salvador has no natural resources, but it does have a boiling tenacity, the energy of its people, the stubbornness in their work, and the hope that tomorrow will be better. Their treasure is the beauty of their land; their fortune is having the *torogoz*.

Finally, the Europeans reached the ravine and took a multitude of photographs, not only of the protruding rock in the middle of the river—the rock that had initially interested Marie and Joseph—but also of the giant rock covered in vegetation.

Both rocks showed signs of damage caused by ignorant townsfolk. On their surfaces, innumerable carvings could be seen. These signs of greed, the Europeans ignored; instead, they started assembling their instruments. While

Joseph and Marie, with a small electric saw, started collecting samples from the uncovered rock, the Dutch mapped the topography. Joseph and Marie took good portions of the red and green veins and the black rings and carefully stored the samples in the containers they had brought exactly for that purpose.

When the Dutch finished their topographical mapping of the ravine, they placed their seismograph sensors, and in that day, at that time, there were no tremors or faults detected. The mapping was extensive and complicated. It was difficult to reconstruct the rock's surface, for as the sensors scanned the surface, they noticed the rock had several peaks and valleys. That's how they realized that the river ran through a small portion of the rock and that the protruding rock, the portion Joseph and Marie saw, was nothing more than a piece of an immense rock.

After several hours of mapping, a probable measurement for the surface of the rock was reached; this included an irregularity in its depth—three meters—which was possible to excavate. It measured 120 meters by 90 meters, or 10,800 square meters on the surface.

After deducing the external limits of the rock, the geologists used their radars to penetrate the ground to map, as well as possible, not only the surface but the depth of the rock inside the guts of the volcano. Their data produced an extraordinary image: the rock was not one rock, but several, all embedded in what looked to have been a fumarole. The space between the rocks supported such a conclusion.

What was even more extraordinary was that the radar could not find the rock's base in the volcano's fumarole because the reach of the radar was a maximum of 120 meters when penetrating solid ground, which meant the base of the rock was even deeper. Another important detail was that the outer edges of the rock or rocks extended vertically down into the depths of the ravine.

In the geologists' minds, a mental image started to take form. They would describe the finding as a rock formation similar to towers, with corridors in between them that extended vertically, from the depths of the volcano and up, until they reached the crater, where they united in a dome that had an irregular surface that measured 120 by 90 meters.

The dome had, according to the measurements of the radar, a thickness of twenty meters, including the three meters that had been excavated to measure the exposed surface of the rock. After those twenty meters, the space between the towers began to be noticed.

The geologists also measured the crater itself, and it had a surface of 220 meters by 170 meters. The volcano's height, from its base to its top, was 620 meters. Therefore, the geologists estimated that the protected area around the volcano should have a radius of five kilometers, the top of the ravine being the center. This would produce a protected area of 90 to 100 square kilometers, to encompass spaces on which rocks containing the precious metal could have fallen when they were spit into space by the titanic forces of the volcanic eruption a thousand years ago.

But something was yet to be explained. Why was the water at the top of the ravine hot? The geologists found no trace of an underground river in the proximity. The small Chagüite River was formed by little springs that flowed down from the neighboring mountains, but according to the geologists, it was possible that the fumarole or chimney of the old volcano still reached a certain depth in which activity in the magma persisted. This could produce hot vapor that, as it reached the surface, heated the small springs that fed the Chagüite. For the others, this explanation sufficed, for there was no way of corroborating it, and yet it seemed the most plausible conclusion.

Their accumulated data filled the scientists with satisfaction. These were the very statistics that would attract investments from the mining companies and provide the necessary capital for the industrialization of the metal.

Again, Emil was the one to slip away from the group and take several walks in different directions. Finally, after one of them, he declared, "We will need a small artificial lake for mining!"

The Dutch agreed with the idea and decided to mention it in their reports.

Emil continued, "The lake could be filled by the never-ending rain of this country," which made the rest of the team smile.

He had already made note of the small valley near the ravine; at first glance, it seemed to be about 200 meters by 100 meters. This was communicated to the rest of the party, who retraced Emil's steps to examine the valley. They nodded and agreed with his assessment.

Up until then, it was impossible to know if the green- or red-colored veins or the black-colored rings would be found in the depths of the ravine. This was a risk that the companies would have to take. But the geologists' report would include that information. They were already sure that the rock was of volcanic origin, and its characteristics favored the metamorphic type, which is formed in the depths of the earth and then brought to the surface by eruptions or earthquakes. These types of rocks usually contain rare metals, like uranium or plutonium.

The team of experts happily made their way down the ravine. After lunch—soup with *tortas de pescado*, toasted French bread, cucumber salad, and tomato slices with salt, lime juice, and capers—they took a little nap and made plans to visit a neighboring town known for its rooster breeding.

The town had a restaurant with an enormous patio where they kept, in their respective cages, beautiful fighting cocks. Striking, colorful, and bright-feathered, the roosters impressed the Europeans with their elegant frames. They took pictures and videos of the fearsome fighting cocks from El Salvador.

From the restaurant, which was built at the border of a cliff, they admired the scenery. Distant mountains ringed a lake, and the Lempa River trailed through the valley on its way to the Pacific Ocean.

The scientists ordered some bottles of wine and *bocas*[15] made with saltines, *queso petacón,* and olives stuffed with anchovies. The policemen asked for sodas with their lemon cake.

On their way back to town, they decided to dine out and walk to the little restaurant stands sprinkled around the city hall. They savored the *taquitos* of Chino Morataya's stand and paired them with *pupusas de queso con loroco* from La Niña Iselda's stand; they bought the same for the

---

[15] Canapes.

policemen. They all enjoyed a moment of satisfaction for a job well done, delighting in their *taquitos* and surrounded by the hustle-bustle of the townsfolk filling the chairs and tables of all the different *puestos*.

After dinner, the group headed to a nearby *nevería*[16] just in front of the park, where they savored the different flavors of ice cream.

As night descended, they returned home to rest, thanked the officers for their company and help, and got ready to retire. Emil insisted on listening to a CD, Mozart's Flute Quartet No. 1 in D Major, his favorite, which he had brought from Belgium. Actually, Emil played the flute pretty well. Even though halfway through the concert Marie was already sleepy, they all waited respectfully for the last note to fade before they went to bed.

* * *

The morning was cloudy and occasionally rainy, which suited them, for they had started to write their reports for the executive board. They described in minute detail the ravine and its surroundings so they would miss nothing germane to the research. They emphasized the difficult climb, especially while hauling machinery during inclement weather, and concluded that an adequate road

---

[16] Ice-cream shop.

parallel to the river must be built. This was but one of the logistical problems they reported.

As they listed all the challenges that had to be resolved before mining the metal, they realized the investment costs would be enormous. A successful operation would require the endorsement, contributions, and cooperation from more than one rich government, such as Belgium and Holland. And yet the potential of this new metal had the power to change the entire world's trajectory as far as energy was concerned. The Dutch and the Flemish had no doubts that their reports and data alone would be enough to convince their governments to approve the budget for the project.

After thinking about it, the Europeans wrote a letter to the president of El Salvador, suggesting he immediately declare El Salvador's sovereignty over the ravine, the Cha-güite River, and the entire volcano. That way, the entire zone would be protected from any intruder, including other governments, who eventually would hear about this discovery. They also suggested he make liberal use of the nation's right of eminent domain to buy, at a fair price, the land surrounding the volcano, which would encompass at least a thousand-meter radius around the base of the volcano, and declare a "zone protected from industrialization, commerce, or housing" for at least an area of twenty-five square kilometers around the volcano.

The letter was delivered to the municipality by Emil, accompanied by two officers, who gave it to the mayor. The mayor himself received it, attached the municipality's seal, and assured Emil that the letter would be delivered to the president that very day. The mayor belonged to the same political party as the president, which guaranteed there would be no bureaucratic delays.

A messenger left the municipality with the letter, headed to San Salvador, the capital of El Salvador, with the demand that it be delivered to the secretary of the president of El Salvador.

The day went by with no other news for the Europeans, so they made plans for a second excursion up the ravine the next day. At ten in the morning that next day, a black sedan, followed by a patrol car and a pickup with four soldiers on board, parked in front of the house. From the sedan emerged two middle-aged men and a young woman about thirty years old. Policemen and soldiers took up posts on the four street corners, blocking the flow of traffic as needed. The young woman used the bronze-lion door knocker to let the occupants of the house know they had a visitor.

One of the Dutch geologists opened the door and was taken aback by the official visitors. He let them in, and the woman greeted him in English; she was the translator for the two other men.

The visitors and the scientists all sat around the dinner table, which was big enough for eight to ten people, and the young woman introduced the men as representatives of the president of El Salvador. One of them—a medium-height man with early-stage baldness, horrible glasses, and an unapproachable, serious demeanor—was the country's deputy minister of the interior. The other man was the deputy's opposite—tall, mustache, pronounced lines around the mouth that spoke of good humor and easy smiles, no glasses, abundant salt-and-pepper hair. This was the deputy minister of the Court of Accounts, or treasury, of the Republic of El Salvador and a personal friend of the president, plus a member of his extended family— husband to one of the president's cousins.

This man had brought a very special message to the Europeans. After having read Emil's letter and studied the findings from the first excursion months before, the president of El Salvador had spoken to the Salvadoran ambassador in Brussels. The president affirmed he was thankful for the scientists' diligence. He also sent his congratulations for deciphering the mystery of the Light and offered, on behalf of the government of El Salvador, his support and approval for all their suggestions.

He also promised the capital needed to begin the industrialization of the rock. El Salvador would invest 500 million dollars in return for 50.4 percent ownership in the total project, which would guarantee El Salvador held the majority vote when other nations and private companies joined. Similarly, he assured the scientists that Belgian and Dutch companies in charge of the extraction of the metal would receive the nation's franchise to import the necessary equipment for it.

The deputy minister of the treasury commented that 500 million dollars represented only 25 percent of what three thieving ex-presidents of El Salvador had stolen from the nation's poor; their crimes were known by everyone in the country by now. So far, they could prove that they stole two billion dollars, so investing 500 million in a project that would benefit seven million Salvadorans was not only plausible, but obligatory and necessary. Everything about the project foretold success.

That afternoon, the scientists received an invitation from a family who lived in town. They were the descendants of Swiss pioneers and were known nationally not only for their fortune and philanthropy but for having introduced new technology to the coffee industry, which had greatly increased production and quality. These Swiss descendants invited the Belgian and Dutch to their estate to enjoy the country's typical cuisine. The Europeans accepted the invitation, and the family sent a four-wheel-drive vehicle to pick them up.

The estate was located at the top of the volcano on which the town was built; their land produced the best coffee beans in the region due to its altitude. Maurice, a member of the family, was an engineer and agronomist. He lived in his own home on the estate, taking advantage of the panoramic view the altitude commanded. From his terrace, he could revel in the sight of a row of volcanoes, the town below, the great valley of the Lempa River, a lake in the distance, and various smaller mountains.

Together, they spent a splendid afternoon. Curious, Emil once again explored every corner of his environment. He toured the estate on an all-terrain vehicle the family lent him to accompany Maurice as he showed Emil around.

Emil came back from the excursion laden with guavas, *granadillas*, and ripe mangos, fruits that grew all around the estate. Maurice gifted them several bags of high-altitude coffee harvested from his own estate and packed in the family's factory.

Seeing Emil's childish smile was a pleasure, as was hearing his stories. "I almost fell as I was turning onto one trail!" he explained to his party, who felt a shared sense for envy and regretted not having joined him. They had stayed back, drinking and eating *atole de elote, riguas con queso, lomito* in tamarind sauce, and the legendary *pupusas de chicharrón* and *pupusas de queso con loroco*.

Before nightfall, they went back to their accommodations, happy and thankful for the hospitality, not only from the Swiss family but from the entire country. At home, they continued to expand their reports, and making the most of the afternoon heat, everyone, even Joseph, refreshed themselves in the pool and then rested in the rocking chairs before going to bed.

But the next day came with worries for the group. Marie woke up feeling nauseous and refused to have breakfast. She felt tired, but had no fever. And so the questions began: Had she eaten something that made her ill? Was she bitten by an insect? And other questions of that sort.

They decided to take her to the town's small hospital, which had recently opened. Its name was David King's Hospital, in honor of him and his family from Garden City, New York; they had gifted the land and the hospital for the town's benefit. Their fortune and philanthropy had equipped the hospital with all necessary services and personnel. The hospital had become the focus for the townsfolk's health.

When the Europeans arrived with Marie at David King's Hospital, the waiting room was jam-packed with patients and their families waiting to be seen by a doctor. The officers who accompanied the Europeans hurried forward to ask one of the secretaries to let the director of the hospital know the issue and the patient's importance.

Accompanied by a doctor, the director greeted the Europeans and then led Marie to one of the examination rooms. Two nurses were in the room with the doctor, who ordered preliminary tests, including an abdominal ultrasound. The results came back after a while and were given to the doctor. The doctor read them carefully and invited Joseph, Marie's father, into the examining room where Marie was waiting for news.

Joseph couldn't hide his worry when he was asked by the doctor to follow him. He went pale and became dizzy, so the doctor suggested he sit until he felt better. Joseph regained his composure promptly and followed the doctor.

As he entered the examination room, Marie took note of her father's demeanor and quickly inquired, "Is something wrong?"

The doctor didn't answer right away. After a few moments, he said, "No, Miss Marie, on the contrary. The tests indicate you are pregnant. All of us at David King's Hospital congratulate you."

Marie's and Joseph's faces showed their surprise, but their expressions quickly changed to happiness. Father and daughter shared an embrace, crying and whispering gratefully, "Thank God!"

The rest of the day was hectic. Marie had to make several calls to Belgium to communicate the unexpected, exciting news to her husband and family. Hans, who was driving between Antwerp and Bruges when he received the call, had to stop the car and pull over on the highway to recover from the shock. Then, proceeding home, he had to make many other stops because he couldn't contain his excitement. He even rolled up the car windows to privately scream with pure joy.

The news couldn't be more timely. Hans had just been named the main representative for an important company that worked with diamonds in Antwerp and Bruges. This would allow him to stay in Bruges most of the time, watching his family grow.

On the other hand, Marie was starting to get weird ideas that she shared with her father. One of them, spontaneous and plausible, was the baby possibly being born in El Salvador so he or she would have dual citizenship, Belgian and Salvadoran. Another idea was to convince Hans and Joseph to buy land in El Salvador and build a house they could live in when the dark, cold days of winter reached Northern Europe.

As incredible as it seemed, Joseph nodded when he heard this last idea and even suggested he could kick in some money to buy the property. Emil, who was already in love with the country, was already set on doing the same thing, even though he had not yet let anyone know that he wished to buy land in a nice place to build his house.

Coincidences always occur in multiples, and sometimes they pile up. When Joseph and Marie spoke to Maurice about the pregnancy and their plans to buy land, inquiring if he knew of any real-estate agencies, he gave them a couple of names and invited them to look at a subdivision at about 2,500 feet above sea level and close to the town. He and a friend had bought the land and already secured all the permits necessary to subdivide an old fourteen-acre estate that was close to his own. Joseph and Marie found this amazing, and they agreed to visit the subdivision the next day.

The Europeans' joy flooded the team's accommodations, and the plans to climb the ravine once again turned into plans to return to Belgium to begin conversations with the companies that would be mining the metal. They agreed upon leaving some of their equipment in El Salvador, so they asked for the owners' permission to use the warehouse. They gladly agreed.

The plan was to leave behind one of every instrument. They packed each in plastic wrap and arranged it on the wooden shelves that covered the walls of the warehouse. They then used a padlock to lock the door. One key they gave to Mr. Cruz, the groundskeeper, and asked that he make sure it found its way to the owners.

Marie also asked Maurice for the names of some gynecologists in San Salvador who could monitor her pregnancy. She also asked about a neonatologist for the baby. She worried that a pregnancy at her age, thirty-five, might require special care that she could not find in El Salvador. If so, she would be forced to have the baby in Belgium and not in El Salvador, a country she had come to love.

The next day, at ten in the morning, Maurice waited for the group and their guard with two four-wheel-drive vehicles to take them to the subdivision a few kilometers from the house. He showed Marie the approved land plats, so Emil asked to see them too. This made everyone look at each other silently as their suspicions were confirmed that Emil was planning something.

They all walked the land of the proposed development, admiring the abundant vegetation and the remaining coffee trees that stood as testaments of what the estate had been. Gigantic cashew trees proved the fertility of the land, and their size made the travelers feel small when compared to the scale of living things in this tropical setting.

As he walked the land, Joseph made a mental note that the sign announcing the name of the future development, BerDor, was bad grammar, for he knew that "*verdor*," in Spanish, meant something is green or abundant in vegetation. He asked Maurice about it, and Maurice, smiling, told him the word on the sign was actually a combination of two names, his wife's and his friend's wife's. Coincidentally, together, they formed a word that seemed to refer to greenery.

The trip back to San Salvador was uneventful. The Europeans decided to book rooms in the same hotel that had welcomed them when they arrived. They planned to stay for four or five days so Marie could get in contact with a gynecologist and a neonatologist; plus, to take advantage of that time, they could visit some tourist attractions.

When they arrived at the hotel, they had to part ways with the officers who had escorted them throughout their visit. The travel agency that had offices in that hotel devised an itinerary that included various tourist attractions from which to choose.

That afternoon, thanks to Maurice's connections, Marie had two consultations with doctors who could take charge of her care and the baby's when she came back to El Salvador. She also visited Gynecological Hospital of San Salvador, which she deemed most adequate for the delivery.

After the comings and goings of the medical visits, Joseph and Marie rested in the hotel's lobby, enjoying their view of the beautiful volcano of San Salvador, which was right in front of them. They noticed that the foot of the volcano provided ample evidence of the impertinence of man in their desire to barge in on nature and possess it; houses had been constructed as far up the volcano as was humanly possible.

Emil and the Dutch, sitting in a table beside them, asked for their usual cheese bocas and olives to go with their dearest beer, Stella Artois, which the hotel had taken great care in stocking in sufficient quantities to satisfy the pallets of the Dutch and Belgians.

Joseph joined them while Marie hung back on a couch, contemplating the happiness of her compatriots and categorically refusing to toast with them. She knew about the effects of alcohol on the early divisions of DNA in an embryo. When she was studying biology in her last year of high school, in a school in Bruges, her class experimented with frogs' eggs, injecting them with insignificant quantities of alcohol. She watched as the substance made disastrous changes to the tadpoles. Several were born with no tail; others, only half a brain. So she told her colleagues, "After the baby is born, a dozen bottles of Stella Artois won't be enough."

They all laughed. They were extraordinary companions.

When the five-day stay was up, they went back to Europe—first Amsterdam and finally Brussels—without incident. The Dutch stayed in Amsterdam while Joseph, Emil, and Marie went on to Brussels and from there to

Bruges in a rental car. They arrived home tired, but in good spirits.

Hans couldn't contain his joy when he finally got to hug his wife. As excited as a young child, he led her to a nursery that he had set up and decorated with youthful accents for the baby.

Outwardly, Marie profusely thanked her husband for his efforts. In her mind, though, she told herself she would have to find a way to fix the room without hurting Hans's feelings.

Chapter 3

Final Decisions

The group arrived in Bruges on a Friday and decided to rest for the day. After the necessary nap, Marie told Hans about her plans and showed him BerDor's plat and planned development. He agreed that it made sense.

As they looked through the documentation, they realized that the largest available building site was a corner lot with tall trees and enough land to build houses for both Joseph and them. That very day, they let Joseph know their decision. As expected, Joseph concurred and thanked them for including him in their plans for the future.

Marie called Maurice and expressed her interest in buying the lot. She asked him not to offer it to any other buyers. Maurice happily obliged and recorded his first sale on the land plat of BerDor, writing "SOLD" over their acreage.

The following days, Saturday and Sunday, Joseph, Hans, and Marie got busy shopping in Bruges. The three of them put the finishing touches on the baby's nursery. Some items were still missing, but they could be added later.

It was pleasant to see in Marie the effects of the pregnancy. The notable scientist was now engrossed in the miracle of a new life growing inside her; she already desperately loved the baby. Her smile, the same one she had when she received her first serenade ever, was now a frequent—indeed, almost an everlasting—thank-you to life for the wonderful gift she had been given, which she hoped would be with her until the end of her days on earth.

Monday afternoon, the executive board met. The meeting was expected to last at least three hours, so the university prepared a meal for its board members and guests. Emil and the two Dutch geologists were in their respective places when Marie and Joseph arrived. They greeted each other with enthusiasm and spent a few minutes going over their reports, discussing any issues that may arise. This meeting was important, and the group's nervousness was palpable. Everything depended on the decisions made by the board; it was now in their hands. The scientists had no way of knowing what the university's priorities were, much less if their project was even amongst them.

When the five scientists entered the conference room, most of the board members were already in their seats.

They all said hello, and the chairman showed them to their places at the head of the table. His name was Dr. Frederick Minnen Von Hagen, a German who spoke the Flemish dialect; he had a doctorate in material resistance from the University of Bonn, Germany. He conducted the board meeting with a firm hand, calm demeanor, and the expected German philosophy of "save, save, save."

The Dutch began reporting their findings. A video of the volcano's geography was shown to give the board an idea of its position and surroundings. Their data on the topography of the area, the mapping of the ravine, and the rock was exhaustive, and it seemed to satisfy Dr. Frederick, who made no comments. He was waiting until after the presentations to ask questions, so he made copious notes on the pages of a notepad on his clipboard, as did all the members of the board.

Then came Emil's turn to report his findings, which were also very complete and detailed. He even included insignificant details about his trip to El Salvador as he described his observations of the volcano and the availability of water in the area, which would be essential for mining. His photos of the prodigious birdlife were beautiful and clear and included spectacular zoom shots. As Emil thought, the *torogoz*'s photos, which he purposefully left for the end, evoked awe and admiration, which were reflected on the board members' faces as they contemplated the exquisite beauty of the national bird of El Salvador.

Emil made no comment about the need to take care of the natural habitat of the vulnerable birds, to then preserve the forests of El Salvador, but he did notice that Frederick and the rest of the board members were looking at each other and making notes during his presentation. Then everyone dined during a thirty-minute break before Joseph and Marie's reports.

When it was Marie's turn, everyone rose to congratulate her on the pregnancy. She and her father presented a joint report full of formulas about the origin of the Light and the possibilities that the energy provided by the new metal they had discovered would change forever the trajectory of human life.

As they concluded their more-than-complete report, Dr. Frederick Minnen Von Hagen and the rest of the executive board rose again to applaud the five scientists who had traveled to a strange land to find the origin of certain whispers about a light on the top of a mountain on the outskirts of a remote town in Central America. Because of their scientific curiosity, they had found something incredible, something innovative and lasting, something that could transform the energy dependence of several countries forever.

Finally, the board and everyone else in the room saw an amicable smile dawn on Frederick's face, which filled them with optimism. They took it as a good omen.

At ten o'clock that night, the meeting was over. It was originally scheduled to be over by three in the afternoon, but due to the thoroughness of the detailed reports, it lasted much longer. The board members left the room tired but optimistic; they felt they were already indispensable parts of an extraordinary event, incomparable to any other in modern human history.

Another meeting was scheduled for the following Friday because the scientists were still waiting for information about the first and second orbital levels of the metal's atoms, which would determine what fissionable energy the metal could produce.

* * *

The rest of the week passed uneventfully. Emil invited Joseph, Marie, and Hans to dinner on Wednesday night. They met in a famous restaurant outside of Bruges, which was close to the sea and famous for its seafood cuisine, having even won some awards in the culinary scene.

Emil showed up accompanied by a young woman who was tall and attractive. Her eyes were light-colored, but her skin was olive, which was indicative of Mediterranean lineage. He introduced her as Carmen Elena Pacheco de la Torre, which sparked the curiosity of his friends; they knew there was a street in Bruges called Pacheco, but they didn't inquire about it.

Carmen Elena explained she was a science teacher in a school in the suburbs of Bruges. She had met Emil at an annual school event in which the students' science projects were presented. Emil had a nephew in that school, and Carmen Elena was his teacher. That year, his nephew was awarded the second prize for his project, which mildly irritated Emil, but it turned out to be an opportunity for him when Carmen Elena approached to console him. Emil took advantage of her moment of compassion to invite her to dinner, which was the beginning of a friendship that smelled like a budding romantic relationship.

Joseph and Marie now understood the very obvious reason for Emil to ask for the development plans of BerDor, the reason was beautiful and had a name: Carmen Elena Pacheco de la Torre.

* * *

Friday finally dawned and, with it, the day of the next meeting with the executive board of Bruges University. It was scheduled for ten in the morning. Joseph, Emil, and Marie were punctual, and they took their respective seats. All the board members were present, but the two Dutch geologists were absent; they hadn't been invited. And yet, in the room were five people unknown to Joseph, Emil, and Marie. The newcomers were invited by Frederick, who now introduced them. Three of them were German businessmen from the industrial city of Dusseldorf and had interests in mining companies from Africa. The remaining two were CEOs of mining companies, one of them Dutch and the other Belgian-French, meaning from South Belgium.

After the introductions, Frederick announced the reason for the meeting, which portended good news. He reopened the conference room's door and invited three people to enter. Each carried a bulky portfolio, presumably filled with documents related to the latest scientific data on the metal, for the three of them were physicochemists from the University of Brussels. Again there were introductions, and then Frederick asked the physicochemists to present their findings. Everyone in the room was anxious to hear the news about the metal.

This first presenter thoroughly explained favorable findings about the metal. His team had found fissionable isotopes in approximately 3.7 to 4.1 percent of the rock's first and second energy levels, meaning the first and second orbitals and three suborbitals, which were verifiable by physicochemical techniques. The fissionable isotopes, however, could only be found in the so-called black rings of the rock.

The second report was a bit more confusing. The metal had qualities never seen before in heavy metals, and these were located in the veins of the rock, which were an inclusive part of the metal and in direct contact with the isotopes. In repeated studies of samples from the three sections of the metal, it was observed that the fissionable particles in the black metal seemed to be absorbed by the green metal and with less intensity by the red one.

"Self-renewable" was the term the presenter used to explain the favorable phenomenon. But he couldn't clearly answer a couple of questions regarding the loss of mass, which were posed by Marie: When any isotope of a metal shifts energy level, it releases energy as it loses mass. So why, in the case of this metal, did the isotope remain near the black ring without acting as a catalyst for its own progressive disintegration, as any other radioactive isotope would do?

That question seemed to be answered by the third presenter, a middle-aged man who was rubicund and had auburn hair; he was probably Flemish. He explained in more minute detail about the metal. Its atomic number was 120, which meant it was a superheavy element and therefore outside the periodic table and deserving of the name Unundectium. Its mass number was enormous, 299, and its fissionable isotopes were calculated at 293.3. The half-life of the isotope was calculated to be between 120 and 132 years, which made the metal ideal for nuclear energy plants. Its use would reduce significantly the cost of the breeder reactors because it was capable of reusing its lost mass.

This scientist suggested bombardment of the isotopes with the commonly used cadmium neutrons until the metal's potential use for energy production was established. That approach seemed very logical to all present. Even Emil, always contradictory, agreed. "Lenkanium" was the name for the new metal that would be introduced at future science conferences in Europe and North America.

After the three presentations, they all moved into an adjacent room to have a light meal, and then the men from Brussels said goodbye and returned to the capital. The remaining meeting attendees returned to the conference room and took their respective seats.

Frederick spoke again and explained to the five businessmen the rules and restrictions imposed by the government of El Salvador and approved by the Bruges University. These norms were directed at any mining companies showing an interest in the industrialization of the new metal.

First, he explained that El Salvador was the owner of the 50.4 percent of the metal and total returns obtained through industrialization or use of the metal in any form.

That left 49.6 percent, which would be available for purchase at a price to be determined by the government of El Salvador. Yet, according to the agreements made and approved by the leaders of El Salvador, it was Belgium's and the Netherlands' right to choose one partner each from any country, as long as they met all the requirements to enter into such a business; their choices would not be contested.

Similarly, only the executive board of Bruges University could name, reject, or accept all other companies from Belgium, Netherlands, or some third country.

In honor of the three Germans with whom he had worked successfully, Frederick suggested that Germany be the third country, for, as he explained, Germany had fulfilled for the last seventy years all the conditions imposed upon it by El Salvador.

The restrictions proposed for the extraction, production, and uses of the metal were as follows:

A. *The metal would only be used for peaceful ends.*

B. *Not a single gram of metal could be sold to countries with violent tendencies that resulted in disaster, such as invasions, thefts of resources, destruction of cities with the objective to spread terror or misery.*

C. *The metal couldn't be sold to countries that either openly or covertly covered for, helped, sided with, or maintained groups or associations with a history of terrorism.*

D. *The mining companies could not apply to the stock market of any country for an IPO, initial public offering, with the intention of selling shares or generating capital for the benefit of its investors.*

These restrictions were slowly and clearly read to the representatives of the mining companies, and they agreed with nods to all terms.

The value placed on the 49.6 percent share of the metal was eleven billion dollars, from which one billion was to be paid to Bruges University; the other ten billion, to the National Citizen Fund of El Salvador, an entity formed by the government to make sure all future earnings were kept separate from the national treasury. The National Citizen Fund would start by acquiring treasury notes or dollars from the United States of America, which would be deposited, stored in, and managed by a bank of that country at an annual interest rate of 2 percent. The idea was to create a citizen fund like Norway's, which, for the moment and, thanks to the earnings from the sale of petroleum extracted from reserves in the North Sea, already amounted to 2.3 trillion dollars, money that Norway's government used solely for its citizens, giving them health, job, education, and social security benefits from the time they were born until they died. Who would argue that El Salvador did not have the right to aspire to the same goals for its citizens? Time would demonstrate otherwise.

Frederick suggested that Germany buy 9.6 percent; Belgium and the Netherlands, 20 percent each. The mining companies of those countries accepted the terms and conditions and decided, that very day, to make their respective payments and deposits in favor of Bruges University and the National Citizen Fund of El Salvador. Representatives of the Salvadoran embassy in Brussels would be called the next business day to have them come to the university to receive the funds.

Satisfied at having achieved the desired results, Frederick smiled reservedly and asked the board for a minute of their attention. He then pulled out of his pocket a letter from the president of El Salvador to the members of the board. The letter outlined what El Salvador was offering to the rest of the world.

It was simple: the unique and admirable qualities of the metal would be used for the benefit and survival of all mankind on our beautiful planet. It would never be used for the construction of arms or to exalt the arrogance and violence of countries who had no respect for human life and who acted with impunity. Respect for life and everything it gives us would be the signature of this precious metal, its seal on every agreement for a quantity of it, no matter how small or seemingly insignificant.

This was the promise made by the president of El Salvador to the board. A promise that was celebrated by everyone, for it came from the representative of a small country that did not bring to the table any selfishness or greed related to the new fortune found in his country. The president was willing to share this fortune with the rest of humanity.

When the meeting was over, Frederick called the president on the phone to let him know the results of the meeting. He also told the president he would be immensely honored to meet him in person. In reply, he was promised an invitation for him and everyone in the meeting, including the businessmen, to officially visit El Salvador. Frederick was sincerely grateful, and when the call was over, he let those present know about the pending invitation.

Before the meeting was officially over, Frederick invited those present to ask questions or suggest anything they wished. Emil had been waiting for this moment. With his usual panache, he addressed the businessmen and explained his main points of concern.

He explained the need to protect the habitat of the innumerable creatures that lived in the ravine, and for that very reason, the street to access the rock shouldn't be wider than two and a half meters. Also, asphalt couldn't be used; instead, cobblestones should pave the road. The vehicles that accessed the ravine should be small trucks—for example, those used in Italy and Spain—only one meter wide, to leave space between each truck and the surrounding foliage, as they encountered each other, one going down and the other up. All vehicles using the new road should be four-wheel drive, have three- or four-cylinder engines and beds with tall sides to accommodate the loading of as much material as possible. The fence that separated the road from the river should be made of stone, a meter tall, so it wouldn't interfere too much with the movements of the fauna native to the area. Et cetera, et cetera.

The businessmen listened to Emil with kind smiles on their faces and promised to implement his suggestions. They expressed doubts about the location proposed for the laboratories that would process the metal. It was Emil, again, who explained that, a thousand meters from the foot of the volcano, there was a small valley in which a man-made lake was being constructed to provide water to the mining companies. He suggested the laboratories be built on this flat section of land near the lake. Of course, another road, similar to the one that would border the Chagüite River, would be necessary from the top of the volcano to the valley; the two roads would meet at the top of the volcano.

The businessmen found this idea excellent, and they agreed to contact the ministers of the interior and public works in El Salvador to plan the road for access to the man-made lake and future buildings that would house the offices, laboratories, workshops, etc., from each company. They also promised to reinforce the Marie Pilar Bridge so that it could sustain the weight of the heavy equipment and trucks laden with mined rock.

Various other concerns and questions were expressed by the businessmen and addressed by the board according to the expertise of each member. Though many questions were left unanswered, everyone was assured that, in time, as things became more clear, all issues would be resolved.

Everyone left the meeting looking satisfied, as if they had gone above and beyond in fulfilling their obligations. Emil, Joseph, and Marie headed to their respective homes to plan their next trip to El Salvador.

* * *

Everything was happening at a seemingly dizzying pace. The mining companies made contact with the necessary authorities in El Salvador to obtain visas for their workers and the permits to import the mining equipment. The

Salvadoran government bought a hundred square kilometers of the land suggested by the Dutch geologists.

Construction of the lake started in the valley chosen, as well as the road up to the ravine, just as Emil suggested—made of cobblestone and two and a half meters wide. The town received a considerable subsidy to cover the costs of building the road that would border the Chagüite, starting from the Marie Pilar Bridge to the top of the ravine; again, Emil's instructions were followed to the letter, even to the extent of having the two roads join at the top and connecting one to the man-made lake.

Other construction work was also being done, such as reinforcing the foundations of the bridge and strengthening the balustrade and handrail. It was also being painted white, and the young women's faces that decorated the bridge's main archway were enhanced. In the middle of the road that ran through the bridge, small, round columns of iron and cement, one meter tall, twenty centimeters in diameter, were set two meters apart and painted yellow; they were constructed to divide traffic and block the way for vehicles other than the small trucks used by the mining companies. Platforms or sidewalks were built all along the bridge and were twenty-five centimeters tall to prevent any vehicle from driving on them. Their spacing was such that the street between the sidewalks was exactly two and a half meters wide, meaning that the bridge would only be able to be crossed by pedestrians, bicycles, and the small construction and mining trucks.

The number of workers needed for the project constantly rose, and a way to house them was needed. The town was slowly being flooded by these workers who came from neighboring and far-off towns.

Government researchers studied the situation and found that the town's aquifer and natural sources for water could not sustain a population greater than 50,000 people. Then, the results of a census revealed the town already had 26,300 permanent residents.

This situation forced the mayor and his council to issue an official proclamation that the town's permanent number of residents could not exceed 50,000 people, which meant that a special permit was required in order to construct any type of home within the jurisdictional limits of the town, which could accommodate only an additional 23,700 residents before the legal limit was reached.

The announcement brought an avalanche of requests for permits to construct homes. The first ones to apply were those who had abandoned the town after the devastating earthquake of 1951. The municipality made those requests a priority because many were descendants of the town's founders who had contributed to the history and well-being of the town over many years. The names of these old pioneers were registered with the municipality; their last names headed the waiting list for home construction.

Another difficulty faced by the town was the growing number of homeless shanties in alleyways and on isolated streets. People from far-off towns, all of them poor and in search of work, erected little makeshift lean-tos using sheet metal or cardboard. The neighbors protested because these squatters threw their trash and relieved themselves on the streets, creating a dirty and dangerous environment.

The municipality devised an innovative solution. It severely forced the squatters to clear out, but only after cleaning the streets. Whoever found employment was given a numbered pass that allowed them to occupy any of the available housing units built by the municipality outside of town. Those with no jobs had to leave town, but before they did, they were allowed to register their names and contact information so they could be notified when a job became available.

The future bonanza was already palpable, even to neighboring countries like Guatemala, Honduras, and Belize. So El Salvador's government made an official announcement that workers from those countries could seek citizenship after six months of uninterrupted working and good conduct.

The Salvadoran government's edicts were unusual but fair, honorable and compassionate. They prompted the governments of those countries to call for a meeting with Salvadoran authorities to discuss, seriously, the creation of a Central American Common Market. This would be the first step toward, in the near future, the Central American State Federation—that dream, still distant, of having a common homeland with a capital city spanning Nicaragua's northern region and the shared border with Honduras. It would be isolated from the earthquakes in the south, at 120 kilometers from the Atlantic to protect it from the very frequent hurricanes, and have a country of 526 thousand square kilometers, 55 million inhabitants, two oceans, 4,632 kilometers of coast, never-ending beautiful landscapes, and more. Someone once said—the nobility jumping on the words—that the union of our countries must be constructed on a foundation of truth, cordiality, and mutual respect for our traditions, races, religions. If this unifying of Central America required but one drop of blood from one of our brothers or sisters, then the union wasn't worth it, for a single drop of blood of a compatriot is more valuable than any union.

The first country to send a committee of atomic energy experts was the United States of America, for that country had a special interest in transforming and modernizing their network of providers of electric energy, which they consumed daily in great quantities.

The committee was received by the minister of the interior, and all the requirements to obtain the metal were explained to them. A mutual contract was signed. In addition, the United States asked for another contract to obtain the metal and use it as a source of energy for submarines, aircraft carriers, spaceships, and a nuclear energy plant to be built in a region of the Central Pennsylvania to fulfill the demand for electricity of 400,000 inhabitants.

They were told that their application would be thoroughly studied before a decision was rendered and that it would take no less than three months, no longer than six. They were also informed that the price per gram of the metal's isotope would be no different from the price of the metal that might not contain it. The North Americans gladly agreed to those terms.

The news about the metal and its extraordinary qualities was spreading across the world, and many countries tried to communicate with the ministry of foreign affairs to start the conversation about participation in some way and, with it, the possibility of opening embassies in El Salvador.

The work for the mining companies was going great, and the construction of the artificial lake was about at its midpoint when the lake's christening came up. Someone had already suggested the lake be named something Flemish, which was accepted by the populace, for they did appreciate those three extraordinary human beings who had made the discovery.

Each company's installation was massive and had its own lab to determine the number of fissionable isotopes per gram of metal, and so establish a selling price.

The reserves in favor of the Citizen Fund (ten billion dollars) were gladly announced by the government of El Salvador. Its congress approved the use of 1 percent of the interest for social issues and the modernization and maintenance of hospitals, schools, nursing homes, etc. The other 1 percent was to be used for the continued growth of the fund.

* * *

A house in Bruges was filled with exuberant joy and anticipation for the imminent arrival of a baby. The happy parents, Marie and Hans, were going crazy planning everything to properly welcome their child. An ultrasound of Marie's womb showed the baby was a boy. Further analysis of the amniocentesis proved the baby was totally healthy. The parents had already named the child Robert Gregory, honoring Marie's grandfather and Hans's great-grandfather.

Marie was going into her sixth month and gave no signs of complications. She had continued to work every day at the university and hadn't stopped exercising three times a week. The university, thankful for the millions of dollars it had obtained due to Marie's work and talent, gave Marie a sixteen-month, paid maternity leave with bonuses, health insurance, etc. The costs of all pre- and postpartum procedures would also be covered by them. Joseph was also given a six-month vacation to be used as he pleased.

On a previously agreed-upon date, the birth would be induced at the Gynecological Hospital of San Salvador. The preparations for their return were all finalized. Through a real estate agency in San Salvador, they found a house for rent that Marie found adequate, given its size and comfortable floor plan. It was located in an ideal zone of the city. The contract started a month before the estimated birth date and could be extended for six months after it, with additional opportunities to extend it even more. For as long as they pleased, the colonial house in Jucuapa—the old town on the banks of the ravine and the original site of a strange rock that emanated light—would remain ready and available for use as well.

Construction on what would be their winter house in BerDor was advancing quickly, which brought such palpable joy to Marie, Hans, and Joseph. They were very happy to have made the decision to be a part of the town that had given them an incomparable welcome.

Emil, on the other hand, had made the wise decision to formalize his relationship with Carmen Elena. The wedding would take place ten months after the birth, so Marie and Joseph were able to be the maid of honor and best man, respectively, at their wedding. Emil and Carmen Elena had bought a good-sized estate in BerDor, and they retained the services of the same architect used by Marie and Hans to build their house.

The town was growing fast, projects were approved, and the local population would soon be reaping the benefits. One of these projects was the construction—in an abandoned farm two hundred meters or so below the crater of the volcano, on the other side of the road to *el* Chagüite—of a small lake about 120 meters by 50, and 12 meters deep, which would function as a retention pond for the town. Additionally, though, portions of it would be used as a recreation spot for the townsfolk, as a place to raise tilapia to feed the students of the district, and as a focal point for industrial education.

The little lake would feed on the winter rains and, in the summer, from a pipe system that would come directly from the man-made lake designed by Emil, the biggest in the valley. Fortune favored this lake, for, during its construction, they drilled a well and found a large spring a hundred meters below the surface. Powerful pumps that would propel water to the lake at the top of the ravine were installed.

Next to the lake, over a ten-hectare plot of land, there would be a greenhouse where two million or so little trees of different species would grow to reforest the country and maintain the course of the rivers.

* * *

The birth of Robert Gregory was scheduled for the next year at the beginning of February. The family celebrated Christmas as never before. Close and distant relatives arrived; some they had not seen in years and years.

By early January, Marie and Joseph were back in El Salvador and settled in the rental house in San Salvador. Maurice's family had gifted them a cradle and a very complete wardrobe of baby clothes for a newborn.

During their stay in the capital, they made a couple of trips to the town just to see the progress of the construction on their BerDor house and to be astonished by the changes overtaking the town. They found it completely trash-free, and the cordiality towards them was evident and filled them with warmth. The market was full of vendors and buyers, yet no waste was visible around the fruit and food stands or in the little supermarkets.

Marie and Joseph were more than satisfied by having chosen to construct their home in the town; additionally, Emil and Carmen Elena would be their neighbors. Maybe, someday, they would even get to be godparents to Emil and Carmen Elena's first child.

Hans arrived in El Salvador a week before the eagerly awaited arrival of their son, and the day finally came for inducing labor. There were no difficulties, and Robert Gregory came into the world weighing 3.6 kilograms and with a pair of lungs more strident than an opera singer's. On the birth certificate, Marie decided to use Roberto Gregory as the child's given name, which made Hans smile.

When one of the nurses asked why they decided to have their baby in El Salvador instead of Belgium, Marie, who had secretly studied and learned the guanaco's regional dialect, culture, and traditions gave her the most beautiful, mischievous smile and answered, "Pa' que najca jalvadoreño, pues!"17

---

[17] So he is born Salvadoran!

ABOUT THE HOPELESS WISDOM OF LAS COMADRES

Vocabulary of Las Comadres

In my country, every town has its own *comadres*. In Greek mythology, they were known as the Fates. *Comadres* are enlightened ladies who, as Leon Felipe coined it, *"siempre saben lo esencial."*[18] *Las comadres* have woven, since the beginning of time, the invisible fabric that connects and sustains all people. Theirs is a matriarchal tapestry; the center of the family is the *comadre,* and around her spin the rest.

The *comadre* points out issues and lists the steps that must be taken to prevent the family structure from crumbling. She is a necessary dictator who leads us towards happy endings. We believe that without *las comadres,* there's no family; without family, there's no society; without society, there's no nation; without nation, there's no future.

All *comadres* have supernatural powers. They are in charge of spreading the town's news at an extraordinary speed, faster even than the newspaper, the radio, the

---

[18] Always know the essential.

telephone, and even the television. Really, what they do is use the speed of light to spread *chismes* or *chambres*.[19] More than that, las *comadres* use the speed of thought, faster even than the speed of light, to spread the news.

They are also able to use telepathy to communicate with the *comadres* of other towns. Because—take a moment to really think about it—thought is capable of traveling from one planet to another in less than a second. The same distance takes two minutes or even more if traveling at the speed of light.

Case study

Your neighbor, Toñito Moncada, has been making eyes at Conchita Vaquerano, the *gordinflona*[20] that sells *riguas*[21] and *chicharrones*[22] on the corner by the telegraph office.

One afternoon, Toñito confides in you and confesses this secret passion, asking you to tell no one, which you obviously promise with your heart because you and Toñito are *compadres*; you are the godfather of one of

---

[19] Gossip.

[20] Fat lady.

[21] Tender corn *tortilla*.

[22] Fried pork pieces.

his boys, Ramirito, and even paid for his First Communion party.

That very afternoon, you pay a visit to Licha Cienfuegos, first cousin to the mayor, to order half a dozen *tamales pisques*. Her cooking is so good! She only uses *frijoles sazonados*[23] and the pure *manteca de chancho*.[24]

Licha guarantees her costumers, in a demeaning tone, "I never use *remiendos de babosos*,[25] like the so-called margarine or weird oils made from foreign seeds!"

So, because you and Licha are *cheros*[26]—you graduated from primary school together—and you know she has no phone, you ask her, "*Mirá*,[27] Lichita, can I trust you with a secret? You can't tell anyone."

Licha, who is the consummate *comadre*, repeats the words she has been saying since she was born, "You know you can trust me. I am a tomb, *pues*!"

---

[23] Seasoned beans.

[24] Pig grease.

[25] Fool's patchwork.

[26] Friends.

[27] Here.

And you, now reassured by this promise, tell her all about Toñito's secret, certain that no word of this will ever leave her mouth.

Later, confidently, you head towards Mejías Pharmacy, three blocks from Licha's house, to buy *ganoles* to ease your rheumatism.

As you walk in, the owner, Paquito Mejías, meets you at the door, welcomes you, and asks to have a word in the back of the establishment.

You follow him and sit down in a comfortable armchair in his living room.

Paquito offers you a Coca-Cola that you gladly accept, and *luego, luego*[28] he asks you, "M*irá*, what do you know of what people are saying about your neighbor Toño Mon-cada and *la* Concha Vaquerano?"

When you finish talking to Paquito, you head home and feel that everyone is staring at you as you walk by; they even make faces when they think you can't see them.

When you arrive, your neighbor, Toñito Moncada, is already waiting for you with a sour look on his face,

---

[28] With no hesitation.

and he scolds you, "You…you are worse than a *placera.*[29] You can't be trusted with anything! Everyone is gossiping about the way I make eyes at *la* Concha Vaquerano. I asked you to tell no one!"

And you, all ashamed, tell him that the secret didn't come out of your mouth. It must have been someone else, maybe even Concha herself, who, to feel important, might have told someone, and someone told someone…

But you know. You know exactly who spread the news around town and, therefore, probably around other towns as well.

Comadres don't fool around saying, "If that so-called Pedro Guandique de la O took Mariyita, it is because Mariyita wanted to be taken. If Mariyita is now pregnant with a little creature, living in a *cuzul*[30] there by El Calvario, it is because she wanted to have a little creature, *pues*. And if Toñito Moncada approached Concha Vaquerano's stand with the excuse of buying *riguas* and *chicharrones*, and took the opportunity to give her a couple of compliments, and she, who has never been shy, invited him home for a dinner of *riguas* with *queso* Petacones[31]

---

[29] A vulgar woman.

[30] An unpleasant little house.

[31] Cheese made by Petacones.

and *chipilín* soup,[32] and the dinner went on until it was late for both of them because they lost time 'talking' and then woke up all dazed, and Toñito said that he didn't arrive home until morning because he had to see Tiburcio Malpartida off with a couple of other friends because he was going to join a caravan heading north that departed from San Pedro Sula with the idea of crossing to the *Yunaited*[33] as another immigrant, and Toñito trusted that Tiburcio, who had actually departed two days before and by now was probably already out of the country, in Guatemala, waiting for the caravan, couldn't tell anyone about his little adventure with Concha… Even the police had to be informed about Toñito's disappearance because, as a valuable asset of society, he even was a member of the city council, and the mayor held him in great esteem, for he was one of the only ones who knew how to read, and that wasn't at all on the *comadres*, but on Toñito and Concha for being so mischievous."

About this ability to travel faster than the speed of light, something must be said. If *las comadres* say it, it has no value. But if some old academic says it, then it is recognized as possible.

---

[32] Cheese-and-doughball soup.

[33] The United States.

For example, a *comadre* travels to the edge of the known universe and comes back, in an instant, to finish reading her *novena*.[34]

If she dares talk about this in public, everyone comments, "What a silly lady!"

But, if a quantum physics professor from a renowned university in England, one who has been awarded a Nobel Prize, says, "If I stand on a hill, with nothing hampering my vision, and my vision travels faster than light and goes all the way around the universe, it is very possible that I, at the same time, will see everything that's in front of me as well as what's behind me. So I will be able to see my own occiput, meaning the back of my own head, as well as my nape and my back," then he is seen as a genius.

Really, both *la comadre* and the professor are referring to the same thing. Their thinking is so far ahead of what we currently think are the limits of our physical world. But the limit of thought is willpower and faith, and, actually, thought and faith are one and the same. Without faith, there's no thought; without thought, there's no faith. And without faith, "the mountain won't move."

Las comadres can easily recognize each other, for they are almost always dressed all in black, for they are constantly

---

[34] Religious devotion or prayer ritual lasting nine days.

mourning the death of a relative or close friend, even if they died years ago. When they aren't in black, they dress in long, fluttering robes with embroidered pockets and sleeves. They are in charge of giving nicknames to bad leaders—we have a prodigious supply in our country—and to the other rascals who roam our streets. These nicknames can be perceptive or descriptive, naming a characteristic of the person.

Here are some of the nicknames: *El Mica Polveada*,[35] an old candidate for president; and *El Trompa de Nuégado*,[36] the most recent little thief who stole from the poor and is now hiding in a neighboring country to escape prosecution and humiliation.

And then there's *Toño Sospecha*,[37] an unlucky young man who was caught in the act when, to fight hunger, he stole some hens. As he was being arrested by the police and having his thumbs tied, a couple of chickens hanging from his back, somebody asked, "And why are you being detained, Toño?"

He answered, "Well, I'm a suspect."

---

[35] The Dusty Screen.

[36] The *Nuégado* Mouth (*Nuégado* is a type of fritter from El Salvador.).

[37] Suspicious Toño.

El Casi Tres Onzas[38] is a very accurate nickname given to Casimiro Peñate, the owner of a small general store. He was known for cutting short the yard of the cashmere he sold. This trick cost him a lot of clients, which in turn benefited Víctor Nichárico, a dear Italian man who was neat and honest, intelligent and kind. His store flourished rapidly, and he was able to make enough money to educate his children, one of whom even became a renowned banker. After the earthquake that destroyed the town, Víctor opened a store in the capital, and his fondness for his town moved him to name the store after it.

Casimiro Peñate liked to brag about the gold fillings in almost all of his teeth, saying that it added up to almost three ounces. And that is why he was named *El Casi Tres Onzas*, which was fitting because his name was also *Casi… miro*. *Las comadres* said, if Casimiro smiled in the dark, the gleam off his teeth made him look like an apparition.

Other nicknames that have persisted throughout generations include the one given to the poor young woman who plied the boys of the town with her favors. Eventually, Carmencita, the name of our character, became pregnant. But as it was impossible to tell who was the lucky client, the townsfolk came up with a happy way of answering the question of paternity, which saved some boy from the duties of fatherhood. And so it was agreed that Carmencita

---

[38] The Almost Three Ounces.

would now be called *La Panza de Ocho*,[39] a nickname that, to this day, has not been surpassed by any other girl of the "happy life."

Now, let me tell you about two others. *El Furia* and *La Pe De Be*. Don Elías Sigüenza Macario from the Amapolas village is called *El Furia*[40] because he lives eternally angry. Everything makes him mad, and when he talks to his neighbors, his screaming is heard all the way to San Miguel, where he is known for his temper. *Migueleños*,[41] when they hear distant shouting, simply tell each other, "Don Elías is chatting."

Because it was so hard to get a job in town, don Elías joined a caravan heading to the States. One of his cousins lent him the *pisto*[42] to pay for the *coyotes*,[43] and he was able to enter California as a *mojado*.[44] He had heard that San Francisco was a very pretty city where work could be found. But he found nothing until some drifters offered

---

[39] The Eight's Belly.

[40] The Fury.

[41] People from San Miguel.

[42] Money.

[43] Person who helps illegal immigrants enter the USA.

[44] Immigrant.

him the position of "drug distributor," which he gladly took, thinking that the drugs were aspirins or *ganoles*.

After working for a couple of days, he opened one of the packets and found little plastic bags with white powder in them. Elías tried some of it and almost went mad. When he awoke from a nightmare fueled by the powder, Elías thought to himself, *These* canallas[45] *are killing people!*

So by any means necessary, he returned to his town and opened a shoe stand in the market. He fixes old shoes. Turns out, he has a talent for it; they end up as good as new!

Well, don Elías likes to use words he learns while watching *telenovelas*. That's why he calls all mischievous boys *canallas*, and sometimes he uses entire phrases that he himself doesn't even understand. He once learned the word "therefore," which he heard from a *telenovela* judge who was sending to jail a rascal who had stolen some hens. From then on, don Elías used "therefore" as often as he could, even when he was buying ground coffee in 'Ña[46] Lolita Cuellar's stand; she sells great pre-brewed coffee made from a mix of medium-altitude beans from the Pacheco farm, which is now owned by the Jombers.

---

[45] Bastards.

[46] *Doña*, Mrs., or Madam.

La Concha Vaquerano, the girl who sells *riguas* on the corner near the telegraph office, once asked don Elías for advice. She told him that there was gossip going around about her and Toñito Moncada, and she wanted to know what she could do to make it stop.

Don Elías seized the opportunity and told her, "This is happening because you use *pachuco* dresses and your whale ass shows; *therefore*, what you have to do is desist from using such attire so those selfish *canallas* will use their time on something else."

La Concha, legendary for being dull, understood everything backwards. So she went around wearing her *pachuco* dresses and sometimes even a miniskirt.

Those sly boys, as they saw her coming, hid and shouted at her, "*Pe de be! Pe de be!*" which can only mean *pompis de ballena.*[47]

Now, this has become Concha's name. She thinks it's a complimentary catcall and feels like the prettiest girl, even prettier than Ariadna Welter, the Mexican *chulona*[48] who drives all the boys mad, *pues*.

---

[47] Ass of a whale.

[48] Often nude.

Las comadres lead the *novena* when a friend or relative dies, but they are also in charge of disciplining spoiled children, which requires a stick to hit the most spoiled ones on the back when they run near the *comadres* while they are praying. They use special sticks, preferably branches from the guava tree, for their toughness and flexibility. "So they won't break!" The result is, after one of these blows, you have to behave...or else.

For unknown reasons, the *comadres* have always inspired profound respect; their indomitable spirits when facing life and their refusal to be broken by misfortune are but two of the reasons for that. Their loyalty cannot be bought; they grow and live in poverty. But they always stand firmly in the center of truth, and their knowledge is essential for those around them.

When facing injustice, their faith is always on full display, and their tears can never be bought. The truth in their motives, as they walk the paths of life, can be perceived in the eloquence of their silence and in the pauses of their steps, in their silent strides, blunt responses, and calm laughter.

Bicoin[49]

'*Nas tardes*,[50] 'Ña Licha."

"'*Nas tardes*, 'Ña Tenchi."

"Tell me, 'Ña Licha, you who reads the paper, you who even subscribes to the paper, what do you think about the new *pisto*,[51] that so-called *bicoin*? 'Cause, to be honest, it has me bewildered and even worried. You?"

"Well, 'Ña Tenchi, to us who trade in the minor league—like you with your bakery and me with my green mangos and Hass avocados—well, it doesn't really affect us. *Bicoin* is for big-time deals; let's say a hundred dollars and up. 'Cause, notice this, how am I supposed to give change to a buyer that has only asked for half a dozen mangos when he is paying me with a single coin that's worth a thousand dollars? Where would I be getting the *pisto* for the change, *pues*?

---

[49] Bitcoin.

[50] *Buenas tardes*. Good afternoon.

[51] Money.

"In your case, even if you're selling a dozen French loafs or a dozen little pineapple cakes, you would have to sell your house, bakery included, to give back the change to a buyer using *bicoin*.

"For now, the government will be giving us, each citizen, an account with three hundred dollars in *bicoin* so we can make little trades, and the bank will keep up with each account balance 'til we run out of *bicoin* or we make our own deposits to keep trading.

"'Ña Corina's kids are very smart with their phones; they showed me how to buy and sell with *bicoins* using my cell phone. I got a headache just trying to learn, but one does eventually learn, step by step, and suddenly the process is easy.

"They're saying that the government is even planning to create a whole town devoted only to manufacturing *bicoins*. Yes, they'll be using one of the volcanoes as a furnace to turn the smoke into energy to be able to move the machinery that produces *bicoin*. Right now, only in Japan they know how to. Imagine, 'Ña Tenchi, our dear little country producing *bicoins*, *pues*!

"Do the math: a quintal of coffee is worth two hundred dollars, and a whole farm is needed to actually profit from it. But with a single *bicoin* coin, you can make big-time profit! It would be like having three big farms, each producing a hundred quintals. Only the Jombers could do that.

"But, well, 'Ña Tenchi, I think *bicoin* will really help us if our leaders don't decide to pocket the profit to buy little houses all around the *Los Yunaites* and the *Parises*.[52] But if we are lucky, and we get some honest leaders, well, we can progress as we all hope to."

"'Ña Licha, thank you for this conversation. *Orita*,[53] I'm going to contact Corinita's children so they can teach me all about making money with *bicoin*."

---

[52] Paris.

[53] Right now, with haste.

The Prophet

'Nos días,[54] *'*Ña Licha."

*"'Nos días, '*Ña Quetiya."

"Tell us, 'Ña Licha, you who just learned to read, what is a prophet, *pues*? 'Cause I've been hearing the priest talking about prophets in his Sunday sermons."

"Pues mire,[55] *'*Ña Quetiya, a prophet is someone who says what's going to happen a couple of days before it happens. For example, Lucho Menjívar. People say he is a prophet 'cause he knew that Pedro Guandique was going to take Mariyita—that girl, 'Ña Corina's daughter, the one that works at Mejías Pharmacy selling lollipops, *ganoles*, and aspirin… Well, Lucho told some people, *'Ese*[56] Pedro is going to take Mariyita,' and so it was that *el* Pedro took her. Now she's all pregnant and living in a *cuzul* near El Calvario, living in sin. They don't even attend church.

---

[54] *Buenos días.* Good morning.

[55] Well, look.

[56] That.

And there you have him, Lucho, going all around, saying, 'Didn't I tell you about Pedro and Mariyita?'

"That's why they say that he's a prophet, and Lucho, after seeing some paintings of prophets, all of them long-bearded men, is letting his beard grow long so he will look like them. But his beard is sparse, not close to being as full as the prophets'. And Lucho doesn't even take care of his. When he drinks *atole de elote*,[57] all of it gets stained and on he goes, all dirty and with his beard full of *atole*.

"So, 'Ña Quetiya, that's a prophet. The one who says what's going to happen a couple of days before it happens."

---

[57] Drink made with tender corn.

Lazarus

'Nas tardes, 'Ña Licha."

"'Nas tardes, Carlotiya."

"Look, 'Ña Licha, today the priest said something about a so-called Lazarus that was very dead when Jesus came and just took the death right out of him. Do you know anything about this?"

"Well, Carlotiya, I understand Jesus was always helping people. Once, this relative of his, Lazarus, was hit by a sickness, and medicine wasn't being effective, so he expired. Then, all dead, they put him in a cave because that's what they used to do with dead people, *pues*. And so, just before that, they had to let Jesus know—he was going around to other villages—that his relative was very sick, tremendous fevers, something like malaria, and that Lazarus's sister was inconsolable.

"And so Jesus made his way to Lazarus's village, but he was too late. Four days it took him to arrive, for there were no taxis back then, and when he finally did, well, Lazarus was very dead, three days dead, and buried in the cave, stinking.

"The sister cried and cried and told Jesus, 'Why weren't you here earlier? My brother would still be alive, *pues*!'

"Jesus told her, 'Stop crying, Martita.'" That was her name. "'Imma help you. Take me to the cave, and I'll ask my dad for a hand, You'll see; everything will turn out okay, but stop crying. You're getting on my nerves.'

"Martita took him to the cave, and it smelled really, really bad, full of flies all around, even inside. God knows how they got in.

"So Jesus told Peter, who was with him, 'Look, Peter, lend me your handkerchief. I need to cover my nose; I'm getting nauseous.' And Peter handed him the handkerchief to stop the smell from piercing his nose and making him nauseous, but then Jesus said, 'Wouldn't you have another one, *pues*? This one stinks even more than the cave!' And so Jesus had to cover his nostrils with his own two fingers, and he told two bros that were around, 'Move this stone. I want to talk to Lazarus!'

"They laughed because they knew that Lazarus was already dead, four days dead, but still they moved the stone, and the cave was left wide-open.

"And Jesus stood in the entrance and shouted, 'Lazarus, Lazarus, it's me! Wake up. I wanna speak to you! Get out of this awful cave they've jammed you in.'

"And you wouldn't believe! Lazarus rose from the ground where he was laying, and he started to walk out of the cave, towards Jesus, who was calling him. He looked like one of those mummies in El Gordo y el Flaco[58] movies, all patched up, walking so slow yet always catching Gordo though Gordo is running, running, running with his little legs and his big belly. Well, Lazarus looked like those mummies, all wrapped up in bandages, and when the bros that moved the stone and the rest of the townsfolk around saw him, they all ran for it, stepping on each other, *pues*, so scared about seeing death coming for them.

"But Jesus told him, 'Remove those bandages, Lazarus; you look like a mummy. You are scaring people! And even those *chuchos*.' There were some dogs hanging around that now were barking and howling like crazy.

"Lazarus tears off the bandages from his face. He couldn't even see, and it would be dangerous if he fell because of the rocks on the cave's floor. And so he exited, and under the bandages, he was just as he was before dying.

"So many of the runners came back to see the marvel and thank Jesus.

---

[58] Laurel and Hardy, the British-American comedy duo.

"Jesus asked Lazarus as soon as he was out of the cave, 'And how are you feeling, then?'

"And he answered, '*Pues aquí,*[59] a bit dizzy, man. I was very cool, playing cards with the bros, when you called me, and because you are my relative, well, I had to come to see what you needed. But as I was walking towards you, I thought, *Well, what does he want with me that he needs to resuscitate me if I'm gonna die anyway?*"

"'For now, stop thinking about that, and go console your sister; she hasn't stopped crying. Also, ask her to make something to eat. We haven't had a proper meal in a while; we were rushing to come see you.'

"And so Lazarus went to meet Martita, and she made lunch for Jesus and his twelve bros.

"One of her friends told Martita, 'Notice, Martita, that one is Judas Iscariot. Don't feed him. I don't like him; he thinks he's so cheeky, but he's old, and he stinks of *zopilote* and wet *chucho.*'

"But Martita scolded her, 'Don't be like that, Fátima; we must treat everybody as equals, even if they are cunning and rude, like Judas. Also, please start wearing

---

[59] Hanging.

decent clothes; your calf is showing like those ladies in Hollywood!'

"In those days, skirts were very long; they touched the ground, and the hems were always dirty because the ladies cleaned the streets as they walked. But Fátima was flirty, and she liked to pull up her skirt to show her feet with her painted nails.

"Martita and her friends made a lentil-and-goat stew. Very tasty! And so everybody ate—very cool—celebrating that Lazarus was no longer dead. They even broke open a piñata for the kids in the village, and for dessert, they ordered *buñuelos* and baklava to be brought from a Greek bakery in the village.

"Those Greeks, they don't mess around, Carlotiya. As soon as they heard the Hebrews were going to a place where milk and honey abound, well, they took their things and followed them from Athens. And the first thing they did, as soon as they reached the Promised Land, was open bakeries to sell their *buñuelos* and baklava.

"All the while, Fátima was monitoring Judas, and when he rose to pour more stew in his plate, Fátima quickly took the pot so he couldn't. They said he was a glutton, cunning, a thief that took the *pisto* from the communal funds they used to buy lunch when traveling from village to village with Jesus.

"As they finished lunch, they asked Jesus to say a word, and so he gave them a sermon, a short one but a good one. As always, he finished it by saying, 'Behave, or you'll be taken by *el chamuco*,' which is a name for the devil.

"Jesus then complimented and thanked Martita for the food. He said, 'That stew was delicious! And that goat meat...wow! How do you make it so tender? You need to give the recipe to James.' He was the cook of the group. 'His is always tough, as tough as a shoe.'

"Just then, Judas arrived, for he had heard the rumors about his cousin's wedding, where Jesus turned several jugs of water—when there was no more wine because some rascals that invited themselves to the party had drunk it all—into wine. So Judas, fond of partying too, told Jesus, 'Hey, do you want me to bring some jugs of water so we can drink that wine that only you know how to make?'

"Jesus only smiled. 'It'd be better if you sat down and stopped bothering me.'

"'Well, thank you for the food,' Jesus said to Martita, 'but we gotta go. It's getting late, and there are other villages I want to visit.'

"Martita answered, 'What about some stew for the road? I'll pack you some flour tortillas in case you get hungry.'

"But Jesus politely declined, and he repeated his famous words, 'A man can't live only on stew!'

"As they left, everyone started wondering, 'And, well, what's gonna happen to Lazarus?' 'Will he re-die?'

"And so they say that Lazarus never died again; he roams the world waiting for his bro Jesus to call him again. Others say that he did die, but this time around, Jesus didn't raise him because he doesn't like to resuscitate someone twice.

"Others even say that Jesus had to be very specific when calling Lazarus back from the dead, to be sure he only raised Lazarus, not all the others in their tombs, even those creatures they call dinosaurs. But, go figure, Carlotiya, what would we do with so many walking dead and with those wild animals that eat more than Rigo Viñegas, that man that sells tamales in the market, *pues*?"

God

'Nas tardes, 'Ña Licha."

"'Nas tardes, 'Ña Quetiya."

"*Mire*, 'Ña Licha, you who always attend Mass, why is God called God, *pues*?"

"Mire, 'Ña Quetiya, according to the priest who studied in Spain, God has no name, *veá*?[60] But he allows himself to be called that so we don't get confused with some other evil creatures, *veá*?

"Well, the priest says that one day, a long time ago, a bearded man was herding cows and sheep, there around Egypt, when he saw a wasteland burning, and the fire wouldn't stop. This so-called Moses—that was his name—started to panic, telling himself, 'Well, why isn't the fire in this wasteland subsiding? The fire has been burning for an hour, and there was no end in sight.' Moses, a very curious man, approached the fire slowly, trying not to get burned.

---

[60] *Verdad?* Right?

"When, suddenly—can you imagine?—a voice comes out of the wasteland, and the voice says to Moses, 'Moses, Moses! Do not be afraid; don't run. I'm not gonna hurt you. Calm down and stay put; you could get burned, and I have something to say to you.'

"Moses, all dizzy by the fright, asked the voice, 'And who are you, *pues*? And what's your name? And where do you live?'

"The voice answered, 'Aren't you inquisitive. I have no name. If I had a name, like you, I would stop being what I am. And, well, I am who I am, and that's it. Now, pay attention, for I will give you two bricks of pumice stone so you are able to carry them. Give them to your tribe so they then follow the rules Imma write on them.'

"And Moses, with his knees all shaky... Cause, go figure, 'Ña Quetiya, you see a burning wasteland, flames don't stop, and a voice comes out of it! Well, that's the stuff of nightmares; you could even die of fright!

"Anyway, then Moses told the voice, 'Okay, sir, Imma do what you ask, but if someone inquires about the bricks, what do I say?'

"The voice answered, 'First, climb that hill; it's called Mount Sinai. There I'll give you the engraved bricks, and when they ask you about it, you tell them that YA…WU…AY gave them to you. They'll like that answer.'

"And so he did, *pues*, but first Moses told the voice, 'Look, don't you have something easier for the tongue? 'Cause that name you just gave me is kinda hard to say. I don't think even Chinese people can say it.'

"And it answered, 'Well, call me God then.'

"And the name stuck. Though the priest says that we got stuck with that word because some Greek people that invented some wild, beautiful stories about Zeus[61] got the idea to call him that because it was easier than the one given to Moses. Also, according to him, God lives far, far away, though He always keeps an eye on us, just like parents take care of their children—they like them and make sure nothing bad happens to them.

"Once, this kid called Pedrito got his parents' permission to go visit God's place because he had leukemia, and He welcomed him with a piñata and some strawberry-and-cream ice pops. Delicious they were! And then He introduced His son to him and told him, 'Look, Pedrito,

---

[61] Though this is the case for the Spanish, *"Dios"* comes from *"Theo,"* which comes from *"Zeus,"* it isn't the case for the English *"God,"* which may derive from the German *"Gott."*

this is My son, and He looks like Me, and in Him is all My grace. And around here's this dove flying around, and it's also mine; it's very well trained to do whatever I say.'

"And suddenly a white dove appears, and it perches on His shoulder, like a festival parrot! And it whispers in His ear God knows what!

"And Pedrito gets a sudden urge to play with the dove, *pues*, cause it is so pretty, so tame.

"God goes tells the dove, 'Go play with Pedrito, *pues*!'

"And so, the dove played with Pedrito until Pedrito's curfew, and when he returned home, he didn't have leukemia anymore."

THE END

I wish someday that all of us will be given permission to visit Him, the owner of the tamest little dove who loves children, innocents, pacifists who would never think of fighting a war just to get piece of land, those who have never taken a life or sold drugs that push men into a bottomless abyss where they lose their spirits.

About the Sun and the Planets

Cause the atom is not squared, pues!
(elemental physics)

'Nas tardes, 'Ña Licha."

"'Nas tardes, don Julito, how are you?"

"Hanging. With this rheumatism that won't let me sleep. But it's all good. Begging for it not to get worse so I can keep working this life out. I read somewhere that heat is good for rheumatism, so Imma dedicate myself to taking sunbaths every day. That way, I'll feel better. Not even *ganoles* take away the pain now!

"But tell me, 'Ña Licha, you who finished primary school, where did the sun and the planets come from, *pues*?"

"Turcios Aguirre, that so-called wise man, says that they came out of an explosion, a very big one, a lot of years ago. An explosion so loud that it would leave one deaf, *pues,* and stronger than the fireworks they burn in the patron-saint festivals, and he also says that all light came out of that."

"I don't believe it, though. I know he sometimes makes up things just to confuse us."

"I guess."

"So what have you read about the matter? I'd much appreciate your input."

"Well, Julito, many things have been said. Those who claim to know things say that everything had to come out of something, like an explosion, as Turcios says, and that from then on, all things were formed. They said that once, only once in life—and this is what's difficult to get—nothingness itself, nothing else, decided to do something from which everything came. But before that something that came, there was nothing, which means this first nothingness is different from the current nothingness, which means that today's nothingness can't produce anything. Now there's only nothingness, as if it suddenly got bored of creating things.

"What's even more difficult to imagine is what everything came from. What was that something, *pues?* Was it big or small? Square or round? Anyway, others say that yesterday's nothingness is just like today's, meaning that from it there never came anything, not today and not yesterday; if it did, then it would be something, not nothing. And if nothing is nothing, then that something that suddenly appeared didn't really come from another thing, but it actually came from someone that was very bored and decided to do that something from which everything came, *veá*.

"Personally, I believe that everything we see came out of something round, 'cause, if you really think about it, the moon and all the planets are round. And so if they are round, well, there has to be a reason. They didn't come from something square because that would be the best way for them to travel from one place to another.

"This is exactly why I left school; these things give me a headache that not even *ganoles* can cure, and also because Pablito Cienfuegos, my husband, was urging me to marry him. So I decided to take care of my stand in the market to sell green mangos and *tamales pisques* with *manteca de chancho*. They are delicious, *pues*!

"What I still don't understand is where does all that sun heat that helps you with your rheumatism and grows the corn and coffee comes from. But then you have that Isaías, the engineer, cousin to Manuel Enrique, the president. He once ordered a block of ice and strawberry and lime syrups to make snow cones for his daughter's birthday. And so they delivered him a block of ice in a *yute* bag, and when he took it out, it burned his fingers, and they even got glued to the ice. From that, Isaías got the idea that the sun, that also burns, well, it must be cold, so cold it burns. He came up with his 'cold sun theory,' and he even took it to the university and did a thesis for his doctorate, but they didn't pay much attention to him because a professor said that, 'Personally, I've never seen a spark or a flame come out of a block of ice, no matter how much you stroke it.' That was the end of the 'cold sun theory' that turned into a relic in his family.

"Others who claim to be wise say that the sun is a big ball of iron that was formed after the so-called first explosion, and that it is very hot, flames even come out of it, and those flames reach us and keep us warm and ease our rheumatism. But, 'cause no one has been to the sun and brought back a piece of it to be studied by students, then we have to believe this. Tricksters say that for traveling to the sun, one must travel by night so as not to get burned, and only then can they take a piece of it and bring it back so the university can study it.

"But, to me, that sounds ridiculous. The *Migueleño* who says that doesn't even have a job, and he runs around claiming he is a football player for the Aspirantes[62] team, but he doesn't even score. For me, an ignorant, all this marvel that we see must come from another marvel, a bigger marvel."

---

[62] Aspirants or applicants.

Jucuapa's Cinema

Movies used to be divided into specific categories: war, cowboy, *Gordo y el Flaco*, Cantinflas, *guampire*,[63] or romance. Children could go to the movies and see any of them, but never a romance, for this meant a total abandonment of the tribe's rules and, eventually, the punishment of being alone in street games. The youth of the town grew and had fun in the streets.

On a day like any other, a new category of movie appeared: *lucha libre*[64] with wrestlers fighting *la momia*[65] or *las mujeres guampiro*.[66] They used flying kicks and Nelson holds to force into submission the creatures from another world.

Watching El Santo and Huracán Ramírez join forces and use acrobatics to defeat those fanged women or

---

[63] Vampire.

[64] Professional wrestling.

[65] The mummy.

[66] The vampire women.

drive a wooden stick into their chests *pa' que aprendan*[67] was a pleasure.

Later came other wrestlers, heroes like Tonina Jackson, a fat man who could pick up four men at once. Another one was Tamakún, *el vengador errante*, a turbaned brown man who wore diapers instead of underwear. It must have been to keep people wondering what would happen if the diaper came undone while he was executing flying kicks. They all went down in history, and many other heroes followed in their wake to ignite the town youths' desire to imitate them.

The movie theater was a wooden shed on a corner across from the park. They announced the box office was open by using "Marcha de Gerardo Barrios," and at the beginning of the movie, "La Marcha de Zacatecas."

The kids who played in the park waited for the "March" to play before they stopped messing around and ran to the cinema to pay the ten cents each for their tickets to sit on the wood benches and shout, "*Etiqueta blanca!*"[68] asking for the show to start as soon as possible. They also

---

[67] Para que *aprendan*. So they learn their lesson.

[68] White label.

shouted, *"La vieja!"*[69] which evoked a chorus of laughter from the entire cinema.

When the coffins, always hidden in an old castle and occupied by beautifully sinister ladies, appeared on screen, silence flooded the cinema. The most gorgeous of the *guampires*, their queen, was Ariadna Welter, a beautiful Mexican who enjoyed walking around in her lingerie to show off her perfect figure.

The kids who were going through puberty went to the movies only to see beautiful Ariadnita. Their comments were to be expected: *"Achis*! I would totally let her bite my throat as long as she agrees to be my girlfriend!" "That dumb Huracán Ramírez! If he touches my dear Ariadnita, Imma have to give him a hard time!"

When the movie was over, the conversation about *guampires* started. Were they prettier than the Machuca daughters, also pretty and pale, from the other town? To go look at them, you had to bike down the tree-lined avenue until you reached their town. Then you had to sit on park benches for hours in the hopes that one of them would come out of her house just so you could admire and catcall her.

---

[69] The old lady.

There was always mockery when a boy dared say, "Did you see that? She looked at me and even smiled!"

Always, the reply was, "Who would even look at you with that flat head you have, *pues*?" Or, "Don't be silly! You are choco[70] and don't even have a bike!"

It was common for one boy with a bike to transport several others when they went on these pilgrimages to catch a sighting of the Machuca daughters. Imagine the bikes, several boys on board, going down the street at full speed, everyone shouting and kicking to soften the jarring of the brakeless bicycle. Fortunately, there were no accidents during those adventures. It was fun watching how, during their trips back home, the kids took turns pushing the bicycle up the street, with the owner always on top, laughing and joking, "This boy can't even push!" "This is the last time we invite you!" "Go tell your mom to feed you better!" "I bet you don't even like girls!" "Your only use is *hacer el mate*."[71] "Next time we won't ride with this fatty!" Amongst others.

---

[70] Boy who wears eyeglasses.

[71] A traditional South American, caffeine-rich infused herbal drink. "Hacer el mate" in El Salvador means "to do something without effort"; it does not apply to the Argentinian beverage.

One day, a day remembered by all as the biggest mockery in the annals of the town's history, a list of the many works that the president at that time had done "in favor of his nation" appeared on the front page of the capital's newspaper. The infamous list also included the prices, in dollars, of each job. And to the town's surprise, the list clearly included Jucuapa's cinema at a price tag of twenty-five thousand dollars.

And so the townsfolk began to wonder, "And where did they build this cinema, *pues*? 'Cause here we've seen no trace of it."

The president who had so proudly made this list of good works done for the sole purpose of "benefiting our people" was Lieutenant Colonel Chebo Sulme, a small rascal, proud looter of our poverty, as evidenced by his boldness in making the list public, a list of works that were bogus, and lies for which the lieutenant colonel was paid dearly by the country and its people.

Chebo Sulme had a wife, as well as a mistress with whom he had a child who looked just like him, so "paternity was beyond reproach." This woman, who lived near Cinco de Noviembre Street was at an advantage because she was both near the presidential house and on the way to the military base El Níspero, which Chebo visited regularly.

The townsfolk, after reading the infamous list, felt neglected; this was true of even those who claimed to be avid supporters of Chebo Sulme's political party. The "Lieutenant Colonel, President of Our Nation" was no more than another thief, a vulgar liar who followed in the footsteps of anyone who came to steal from the already-reduced national treasury and to enjoy doing so with impunity before ending their office on behalf of successive and endless coups d'états by other lieutenant colonels who repeated the cycle, promising both the possible and the impossible and publishing lies to toy with the hopes and dreams of the citizens.

But that cinema, our cinema, the one that was never constructed and yet cost twenty-five thousand dollars, came to be known as the Best Virtual Cinema of El Salvador, meaning a cinema you could see but not touch, one that is there and yet isn't.

About Rocks and Diamonds

Only in a country like ours can common rocks cost more than a diamond. And this statement has been proved by historical facts.

About twenty years ago, when there was little left to steal from the national treasury, a now ex-president and his lackeys came up with an ingenious, though depraved, scheme to line their pockets with everyone else's money—they would incur vast debts and then trick the citizens into assuming this debt personally.

That mafia-like group decided to ask the International Bank for a 200-million-dollar loan to build a hydroelectric plant that would "favor the general public enormously." Pamphlets were printed and distributed. They showed the design for a new dam and put on a show for the citizens to prove that "this government *does* care about the general interest of our people."

A ceremony was planned for the placing of "the first stone of our future hydroelectric dam." The press came—journalists and television networks—as did ministers; the full presidential cabinet; representatives from the International Bank who had made the loan, with a low interest rate; the heads of the majority political party; and a multitude of bootlickers waiting to seize a piece of the new loan...well, the citizens' new debt.

In the midst of all the pomp and circumstance, the ex-president confidently marched, surrounded by an escort of ministers, down an esplanade lined on both sides with attendees.

Workers, by hand and tractor, had built the esplanade especially for this occasion; in order to avoid complicating their lives with reprisals, they covered the earth with small pebbles so that the ex-president and his entourage would not hurt their delicate feet.

Cameras flashed as soon as the procession stepped onto the esplanade and started walking toward the designated spot for the "first stone of the future hydroelectric dam." The ex-president, in his hands, actually was carrying a good-sized common rock that someone had thoroughly cleaned so that the president's ceremonial suit would not get dirty during the event.

Applause and cheers filled the air. Attendees shouted, "Bravo, Mr. President!" "That's how it's done!"

An all-too familiar smug, self-satisfied smile lit up the faces of the ex-president and his entourage as they replied, "'*Chas gracias!*[72] '*Chas gracias!*" with the obligatory handshakes after the ex-president placed the rock.

The ceremony ended with the scheduled press interviews. In a few hours, photos and videos of the ceremony filled the first page of all the national papers and led the TV news segments.

The people, our people, received the news with skepticism and cynicism, yet with kernels of hope that "maybe this is it; perhaps this government *will* do something for us."

The dam was to be constructed in the center of two mountains, where the natural course of the river narrowed, creating the conditions for a good-sized dam at a low price. Months went by after the ceremony of the "first stone," but no new information was disseminated, and no work was commenced on the new dam. Eventually, some journalist snooped around the proposed site, took pictures of some tractors and workers building a wall to direct the flow of the river, which was what you would expect to see at any dam-building site in the world.

---

[72] *Muchas gracias.* Thank you very much.

A full year went by after the ceremony of the "first stone," and there was still no progress on the dam. Government representatives' mouths slowly filled with the usual excuses for why the work on the dam was at a standstill: "At this moment, we are unable to continue because the floods caused by the last hurricane are blocking the way to the construction site." "As of now, we are working on the general budget of the nation and are unable to determine a final result." "We are in the process of renegotiating the national debt to lower the percentage of interest, and so favor the people."

And so, more months went by, and there was still no progress on the dam. By then, the president's term of office was coming to an end, and the campaign for new president was at its height. The candidate from the opposition promised, as an essential element of his campaign, to complete, "as it should be, the hydroelectric dam to bring relief to the people in their quotas for electricity service."

The so-called opposition won the election, and the past president, famous for placing the first stone of the hydroelectric dam, was prosecuted for misappropriating public funds and for illegal enrichment. He was found guilty and imprisoned, where he remains today, paying his debt by doing time.

The new president announced that he would complete the dam and then organized an identical "first stone" ceremony. Everything proceeded just as before: the new president, the new ministers, the new bootlickers hoping for a piece of the new loan the citizens carried on their backs, the new representatives of the International Bank who had approved a new loan "at a low interest rate," the new cheers and applauses, etc., etc.

This second "placing of the first stone of the future" ceremony ended just as the first: with the citizens' never-ending hope that "maybe this is it; this government *will* do something for us."

Months went by. It eventually became known that, this time, the loan the country had asked for, and the International Bank had granted, to complete the dam was reaching the 400 million dollars mark. The disillusionment of the people as they found out about the enormous sum they owed was glossed over by the publication, again, of photos showing some tractors and workers very, very busy "completing exemplary work that would favor a thousand Salvadoran families and, in short, bring profits to the country, for the excess electricity that the dam would produce would be exported to neighboring countries."

But, just as the first time, months went by without any real progress on the dam. Alarming news about the dam circled around, news that included questions about the whereabouts of those 400 million dollars.

This forced the government to give its people the well-known excuses for the lack of progress. One of them was completely implausible and, though depraved, pretty original and cruel in its shamelessness: the representants said that "the construction of the dam could not be continued because one of the mountains the river ran through had suddenly moved!" And so, they said, it was necessary to wait for the mountain to go back to its original place.

As incredible as it sounds, "geologists of international reputation" showed up, affirming in TV interviews that "it was totally possible that an underground earthquake has moved the mountain from its place" and that, in the future, another underground earthquake could put it back.

Such nonsense couldn't be believed, not even by our national morons. But, as impunity was still king in the national atmosphere, and as the opposition had won most of the seats in the national assembly, protests about the shameless theft amounted to nothing and were finally lost in the pages of the press and in the deafening silence of TV news anchors.

Just as before, the presidential term, five years, ended for that second set of liars, and the now ex-president completed his term of office without ever accounting for those lost 400 million dollars. At the end of his term, without hesitation, he packed his personal belongings—including a twenty-year-old exotic dancer, already pregnant by the dear ex-president—and escaped in order to avoid any questions about his theft.

Another little thief followed this second one—same party, a party that wielded the flag of the deprived, the anxious for relief from deep poverty, the fighters for a fair homeland that already felt cheated by their representatives. His conduct was similar or even identical to "those other corrupt men" who had been defeated in past elections. It reflected the greed of all men in positions of power: forgetting about the one who raised them, concerning themselves with only satisfying their egos, stealing from their own people, burdening them more and more with debt, and pushing them deeper into the misery of countries ruled by tyrants, dictators, liars, and murderers.

Well, our third president launched his campaign promising he *would actually* finish the dam "as it should be." The construction of the dam had "started" ten years ago, and there was no end in sight. The next opposition candidate affirmed that he was totally committed to finishing the dam. He announced to the press that, to do that, he was going to take out a 600-million-dollar loan at a "low interest rate"; this was necessary to "benefit a thousand Salvadoran families," as he had "the duty to bring wellness to his people."

As expected, the opposition candidate won and installed himself in the office of president for a five-year term. This man had been a teacher at a primary school and had personally lived through the rigors of poverty, had been paid a beggar's salary for doing a noble job, but had never heretofore been recognized or compensated well by the arrogant, cunning louts that occupied positions of power in our country.

This man—in reality, an obviously ignorant man—lacked the ability to discuss important issues, even when they required minimum intelligence, and his short speeches caused anxiety in listeners as he misread pre-written, pre-rehearsed scripts and trapped himself due to his limited knowledge and intellect.

Under him, the country drowned in an abyss of poverty and terror due to the lack of economic stimuli and the presence of criminal *maras* that choked merchants and the general public with "security rents"—extortion. During his term of office, the country was awarded the sad title of The Most Dangerous Country in the World.

To dispel the president's reputation for ignorance, the director of the National University of El Salvador and the university's council decided "after a night of partying" to award the president of the country "in all fairness and after a long and thorough examination of the facts" with an honorary doctorate. To prove to the country that this was a well-deserved honor, the university agreed to subject the president to a public mental-acuity exam before the honorary degree was awarded.

Days before the so-called exam, professors of the university warned the president about the question they were going to ask during the exam and requested that he "please, please, please" memorize the answer.

The award ceremony was celebrated in the university's auditorium. There, on the stage, stood our proud president, calm and indisputably distinguished. Before him, a microphone had been set up for the occasion. The auditorium was full of guests.

The director asked for a moment of silence, for it was time for the ceremony to begin. Within moments, the question would be asked and answered, proving to the world how smart our president was.

"What is two plus two plus two minus two?"

The president answered with a triumphant smile on his face, "*Pues*, two!"

The entire audience exploded in deafening applause, and the president thanked them with an even bigger smile.

After the president passed this "very difficult" mental-acuity exam tailored for him with the objective of proving to the world that it was fair to award him an honorary doctorate because he was a "selfless fighter, hero of the poor and the vulnerable," the director of the university addressed the guests and the press. He finished his effusive speech by thanking the world for the honor of awarding the president that very deserving title.

Several ambassadors and consuls attended the ceremony, as well as the complete list of members from the general assembly, the director of the Catholic University, two bishops, and a mob made up of the president's family and friends.

The ceremony began with the beautiful notes of the national anthem, interpreted by the national band of our glorious army, which brought tears to the president's eyes because he only remembered half of the lyrics. When the anthem finally ended, the people at the university's table remained standing, and the director asked the president to approach them.

The president began a slow, distinguished stroll. Moments later, the director of the university extended his arm. In his hand was a leather portfolio containing a piece of parchment; it was the testament to the honor that the National University of El Salvador was granting the very excellent president. It assured anyone who read the parchment that the president was recognized, from that day on and until the end of times, as a distinguished doctor by the university.

Immediately after the president received the parchment, the director helped him into a dark-blue scholar's robe decorated on its borders with a thick strip of sky-blue satin. Finally, on his small head was placed a black mortarboard with a yellow tassel. He was then asked to take a seat in a velvet chair at center stage.

As he sat, the audience stood up and shouted, "*VIVA!*" to the accompaniment of thunderous applause and a hundred different cameras' flashes.

That day, the honored president went back home and, beaming, declared to his wife, "Well, go figure, I am now a doctor!"

Corruption of justice and collusion of the government with the *maras* continued to be evident. The sense of abandonment and disenchantment of the people grew, and the subsequent electoral defeats of the so-called opposition party in power at that time began mining the influence of that administration, forcing the general public to place their hopes somewhere else.

'Ña Merceditas Tovar had been a fierce supporter of the opposition, but her disappointment reached its breaking point when it became known that the candidate for the opposition announced to the press that they had asked for a 600-million-dollar loan to "finalize the construction of the hydroelectric dam."

Merceditas knew that the candidate was planning to campaign in her town, so she designed two banners and planned, with some of her friends, to stand guard in the park's bandstand, where the campaign rally was supposed to be, so the candidate could see her banners. Her banners broadcast the truth and denounced the extended farce being reenacted by president after president who enriched themselves while burdening the people who were forced to carry national debts on their backs. In reality, none of those loans had ever been intended to help finish the dam.

On a Saturday afternoon, the opposition arrived in town with their presidential candidate: the teacher; the eventual president of the country; the poor and ignorant man who didn't even know how to read; the future honorary doctor; the past president's apprentice; the "completer" of the dam, for which he would become the borrower of a 600-million-dollar loan; the traitor to the sentiment of hope of those who fought beside him to give him the power; the man who, against everyone and everything, would place another "first stone" to "complete the hydroelectric dam that would favor a thousand Salvadoran families"; the man who would go down in history as a thief, as another evil, cunning egomaniac; the man who, too, as his presidency was ending, would pack his personal things and hide in a neighboring country to avoid answering to his people.

Merceditas was waiting for him, standing in the bandstand with her two banners and her friends, who were as disappointed as she was with the made-up tales that the opposition and their candidate were disseminating. When the candidate began the meeting by reading his miserable speech, Merceditas and her friends started shouting to get the attention of the attendees, the candidate, and the party, who all turned their heads to look at Merceditas and her friends. They read the banners that they had made as testaments to the truth and to the sadness of their souls. One of the banners read:

NO MORE FARCE!

¡A OTRO CHUCHO CON ESE HUESO![73]

More eloquent, the second one read:

NO MORE FIRST STONES!

---

[73] An idiom that can literally be translated to "To the other dog with that bone," but is similar to "I don't buy it."

The End

As previously mentioned, only in El Salvador can a common rock cost more than a diamond, for, in the construction of the hydroelectrical dam:

The first "first stone" cost 200 million dollars.
The second "first stone" cost 400 million dollars.
The third "first stone" cost 600 million dollars.

LONGINGS

Poems for youth,
when we were able to fight,
as well as forgive.

(1960-1968)

"No llores más,"
rogaron al poeta,
"has llorado ya tanto."
"Mientras quede algo esclavo,
no será mi alma libre,"
contestó, entristecido.

Jorge Enrique Adoum

Lonely Stone

It's you, Lonely Stone,
bitten by time,
where days nest,
days continuous
in their round prints
when they stay behind.
Lonely Stone is a man,
a forehead full of holes
where flowers hide,
insects
that carve
his outline.
And good
and bad,
all will change
but you,
Lonely Stone,
until wind comes
and gets you off the road
when,
Lonely Stone,
you solely serve
as a gravestone.

Preamble

If this is all but the preamble
for a greater war,
why fight then?
If two paths must always be
two separate blazes,
two factions persecuting and insulting,
a winner kills the loser,
enslaves him,
or takes his tongue
so his children can't natively speak
for liberation;
if it all must be but unquenchable revenge,
why fight then?
I won't go with you,
moldy, hateful mob.
I remain
alone,
ashes awaiting resurrection.

Onward

Onward, come on, onward,
bandage your cuts
with the skin of another
and unmake what has been done.
Your company is good,
so disembowel those who adore you not
and unmake what has been done,
even if you have no one beside you
until all centuries die.

Innocence

For bleeding out our own scream
towards the wind
at this hour,
no one can blame us.
If with it,
we are searching for oblivion,
no one can blame us.
To each, their own *sayal*;
their own laughter,
manta, and attire;
their own way to die.
To each, their own furrow
and seed.
To each, their own reap.

Waivers

Once,
we pawned a lonely word
and left
to rescue the martyrs' echo.
Our somersaults
were worthy
of great clowns.
A time for guidelines,
full of black dawns behind bars;
a time for intimate promises
from present men,
most open to oblivion,
to forgetting us,
open to the exertion of being;
a time to carry our tasks in our pockets,
time coming to meet us,
as tricks would a magician.

Last Urge

Standing tall,
no pain in the bones
or water in the body.
Alone,
forever hurt.
Can't remember when!
Fisted decision
in my dirty
hair,
messy…
A child screaming,
breadless,
cold
inside each pore,
through these streets of ours,
so alike…
I'm chained to my shadow.
Since then,
the fight;
since then,
I feel no loneliness…
Should I have to show
truth from the mouth
with this daily setting

that enters my eyes?
Should I bring
a tyrant
and shove our hunger
in his face?
We've wandered this path
before.
Under the sun's dust,
under the dead rain,
under our own stuff,
miserable, unchanged…
Before,
we must give it all
and arrive sweating
to that last minute
of fighting,
where it all shatters
to the grave
and this daily setting.

Testimony

In this our moment,
we must stand
one-faced,
one-placed,
so to leave a trace
of singular voice.
Keep our lover in memory,
trample over what's loved in futility,
fill the pouch
with gifts
for those unseen,
those known,
and empty our hands.

The Echo Ahead

Follow the string that ties befores,
for after is close,
and most are in the signaled
hour
of words
resurrected:
"Ours is the next step,
which will open the path
for life to come into
the sick peasant,
the pariah, the beggar,
the unschooled kid,
the infected poet,
the so-called dream.
Not another step, brother,
for the harvest in the field,
our field,
is bound;
the field tightens
from the fight,
our fight.
Today, more than yesterday, we must
close the door united
in fear,

extend the oasis
of our prime martyr.
The game ends not
with first failure,
and the echo is ahead.
Ours is the next step,
and behind
we've left the grave."

Stillness

Hoarse
from screaming, "I'm not.
I'm not guilty
of either love or fear,
or lying or vicing."
I'm being left
alone and weak
from lifting my voice to the brain
that won't listen,
for it seeks the silence
of an unshattered life.
Screaming is weightless,
and heavy is the voice.
I'm staying still...
now...
Let the beggar be killed,
the sick peasant,
the unschooled kid,
the infected poet.
I'm staying still...
now
with the dream on my back.

Audacity

All was conceived in the voice.
All born from a scream,
transformed into foam.
We haven't wandered
through enough learning
to die
or be silent
in our principle:
"Go on, audacious,
for the echo is ahead!
Leave the present here;
leave the maybe and the possible!
Go on, audacious!
The echo is ahead!"

Retaliation

In our face even,
in our eyes even,
insults won't hurt;
and from these very hands,
retaliation.
Retaliation, yes.
Even if apologies
were promised,
if we've struck our chest, even
three times,
swearing,
to turn the other cheek
once hit.
It's all well.
Retaliation,
knowing our own strength
that from our very hands
must emerge, at last,
retaliation.
Forget not, please,

when retaliation goes,
that others, too,
have eyes and faces,
and hands even,
just as we.

So?

So?
Is it done?
Will it start over?
For a fleeting moment,
an ominous rustling
showed its silhouette
over the petty swarm
of the greedy heritage,
for a fleeting moment…
It starts over;
the earth isn't ours yet,
and seeds
and worms,
all which fought our solitary effort,
it's all ours
in the next step,
all, completely.
Ours is the hymn of the living,
so wield the altar of the fallen,
and sing the freedom of the fight.
For no one will get here,
not the tyrant's gold,
not the dry blood

of our kind.
No one will get here,
and hope
awaits.

Words

It has been spinning
over itself.
What's changed is man;
the rest is nuance
seen by other's eyes.
The stones of a lit-up castle
have been used for the beggar's house;
the torn shirt of the executed martyr
is now paper
daubed of verse,
and the verse
gave life
to verse.
It has been spinning,
without them noticing.

No, No; Yes, Yes

Yes, yes, Mr. Poet,
men, we are dull,
firmly silent on time's nothingness,
solitary boats thrown
by time to a boundless sea,
capriciously.
Journey never-ending.
"There's a harbor waiting…"
Is there a harbor waiting,
lit by a lighthouse
and buoys to mark the way?
No, no, Mr. Poet,
we men are the same, tired of traveling,
ready to lie down on the water,
no longer soldiers,
young old men carrying the torch of tedium
and the pain of loneliness.

Irony

The end is now,
like a wildflower
after outliving
its hope.
It has no mending,
my murky voice;
it is out,
tired of song.
There is no use singing, Mr. Poet!
Voice is unresponsive,
every scream
rehearsed
to fill
our own vacancy,
ever-existing
somewhere.
It has all been cut
at its wake;
nobody will listen,
we are alone,
and now
there is no use.
But tomorrow, Mr. Poet,
tomorrow,
we must start all over.

Escape

"Escaping" is the word
we're bound to say
stealthily;
escaping from the shark,
staying onshore,
watching the everyday dirt,
brothers escaped from reason to be.
Escape oneself;
find oneself different to others.
This calls us to choose
—old calling—
to regenerate new hearts,
escape from open palms
to fisted hands,
as if saying hi
to our nation.

Gambles

The hall opens,
the entrance
where pun enthrones
its farce, its greed.
My metaphorical playing cards:
Let's play the voice
all or nothing;
here go my home and hope,
my vacant stuttering voice,
my vacant voice.
All for a draw.
No money allowed,
no riddles.
Jewelry and castles are not on the line;
we bet on fear and silence,
forgiveness or fury.
All for a draw.
What's your gamble, beggar?
Because cheating
can't dig its nails in anymore.
Let's play for all or nothing,
for man
reduced to a scream
or a single silence.

Arrival

The match was dark,
omens grand,
unforgettable the tweet
of the perplexing happening,
the size of enormity
invincible,
nourished by centuries of stalking for dissolution,
immobility,
thirst for the wait.
We depart
with a knowledge,
a single note
carved in dissension,
and we leave
the clear past,
the underwater treasures,
the burnt willingness
of air
to persist,
declare
that rough step of the tremulous,
those in love with dusk,
the trace of light unshone,
unapparent,

that perhaps wants to teach us,

the new masses,
the new awe for justice,
so to vanish sadness.
And we leave it all.
Alone no more,
carrying the remnants of oblivion
to their dark arrival.
We will enter the right circumstance
that time has laid for us,
the motionless voice of wisdom,
the push of awaited waves,
the mysterious brush to the soul
from arrival.

POETRY OF ABSENCE

I

Your music
is the feeling of distance never-ending;
my solitude's too crowded without your music.
Your music
is the feeling of distance never-ending,
is the feeling of ending, no beginning,
no cease, no limit.
Your music in laughter, voice and cry…
My solitude's too crowded without your music!
My solitude, your music
Get close on a moonless night,
walk close on a moonlit night,
closely watch time's mirror through so many nights.
My dreaming, your music…
Raises my dreaming to look at you, sometimes
and music pours out of the stars,
pours out of any silence.
My dreaming sees you,
touches you
and you've always been far,
always, and now, more than ever.

Eyes in my dreaming can't reach you;
fingers in my dreaming can't touch you...
Eyes in my dreaming!
Fingers in my dreaming!
My solitude's too crowded without your music!

II

Your music
is the feeling of distance never-ending
in your voice and your laughter,
in your brief gait
or your rush.
Your music in the light
omen of your eyes
and in the soft
whisper of your lips;
your music in the wind
that tangles your hair
is the feeling of distance never-ending.
Your music in the name
that sinks in time,
where memory spins.
It is the feeling of distance never-ending
in the faint adventure of your hands
or a past nesting prediction
where a note leaps
of odes primal
to finding a mystery,
its motive;
accompanying your music
is the feeling of distance

never-ending.

III

Hidden image
in a single voice,
always like this,
your dressed voice,
it all,
since harvests of old.
From both of us,
something needs forgetting
for your voice. Bell.
Flowing dragonfly. Laughter. Specter.
Nothing.
I must forget something. Skin only for touching.
White with solitude. Solitude white.
Skin only for touching. For shredding.
For being kissed by an angel.
And I must forget, sacred mouth.
Virgin papyrus. Chalice. Fruit.
Says God's name with no disturbance,
to the end, finished.
Sacred mouth, sacred,
sculpted with love
until birth.
And yet

we must forget.

IV

Whenever you feel like this,
alone,
silent,
thinking about tomorrow's doings,
whenever you embody
a single tear
on your room's window,
or night approaches,
talk
about the places unknown to us.
Together,
it takes you by the hand,
dancing,
to strange places;
close to your mouth,
cleansing your eyes,
touching your hair,
night approaches.
Wrapped, you love it;
named, you smile;
you smile
after crying…

Hypnotized, it steals you...
You come back
not knowing where from,
in love with a second passenger
who turned the tear into a smile,
and
just like that,
no other sound
but your soft walking
gifting your absence
to my young soul
each night you leave.
I say goodbye,
and you look at me not.

V

A slave to the wind
that imprisons your name
between nights,
will surely play catch up with you
and will talk to your ear
about a miserable tree trunk, hurt.
You'll listen, then,
even without me;
nostalgia
will return in an instant,
and again you'll feel it
without me.
It will show your eyes
some carved trunks,
a distant star,
a triangle lost,
a firmament
as a falling bird
shakes its wings
and feels pain
when extending them,
or leaping lines
from a thousand stopped dreams,

Prodigal.
If you could hear it,
echoes would open
those fillers of name,
stubborn in talking,
for they fear getting lost
and are waiting for coming
out as the dream begins,
eternal memory
that fears getting lost,
even lacking a voice
where the dream starts.

VI
Impersonal

Impersonal:
A shaking of the mind,
searching for those pupils
when one must go on in spite of it all,
and everything that's left:
A street full of people
crossing paths and looking at each other,
the wind whispering between the pines,
the river
sheepishly soothing.
Impersonal:
Just like the fight between torn dreams,
no cries,
spring of anguish;
those empty faces,
dull faces.
Impersonal
as faith expiring over sand,
as a goodbye that hides its longing.
Oh, if you only knew

the coming of your soul,
the dying of sadness!
I need you so.
If you only knew
what salt and water
are to a tear!

VII

Learning to have a name
Nostalgia
Distant, alone
Without you, nothing, nothing
Coarse is the word
And to all
Necessary
Towards me
What I touch
Just calling you
Just that
And you don't hear me
As you did
Should we hug
The taste of feeling
And leave it here
Captive
Alone
So you won't return
So you won't return
Alone

Nostalgia
So you won't return
We should shatter
The last breath
The last breath

VIII
I Have One Too

Saliste de mi arco, saeta,
y te fuiste derecha, derecha,
al corazón de una estrella
León Felipe, in his honor

Tomorrow it *will* be here
Seeding the heart
And the belly conceived
And the voice alone.
All tomorrow
And this lingering shadow
Will help me wait.

IX

I sing
for the sleepless ritual of lost time
that leaves a memory,
that leaves a night,
that walks with goodbye.
The never-ending ritual of hours lost!
All things sing
and already in memory wander,
and they all come to pass
even if before they didn't.
You should stay like that,
chant, lost
in the longing to be,
in the knowledge of being
a moment's fortune,
the shadow on a sunken park
that dissolves in silence;
chant, lost…

X

Afternoon and night shadow,
slow and gentle,
of golden rug black
and teary
and nothing.
Oh, absence of shadow and nothing!
Made of satin and lily,
it sways sleepy arms,
longing to be alone and captive
beyond my words.
Take this lyre made of dreams,
this scrap made of stars,
this chained slinger,
this crack in it all.
I'm coming,
warm with your body,
waiting for goodbye at the corner of time,
where a friend waits for you in wrinkled dress,
never worn
beyond your naked body.
Take this mantle of verses;
that place is too cold.

ADVENTURES
IN POETRY

Genius Nameless Poem (1963)

Sweet acanthus ivy,
the Soul
sticking to its body and the sound
born in a sigh,
a sigh of time…
Time is a crack in the hollow
through which the dead walk
when the veil of nothingness tears,
and Soul is but a drop of void,
leaking to the urge of death,
to its dark withdrawal.
Creature's solitude motionless,
tied to touch,
nothingness and time;
constraint, voracious in stature,
which cannot belt all the Soul.
Extending its wings, cut out
by squirls in the air,

hostile to word,
driving the call of insomnia
and exploding the nurturing vein,
it gets lost, mute,
chained to everyday movement
and the dark vault of nothing.
Movement blue, movement
that tears tranquility,
and with it, vanishes!
The pulse that moves it,
the skin that contains it,
bleeding out the altar, the prison,
filters through a tear,
a blurry pain that can't be felt.
The clear spot of an Idea.
Together they come; they merge
with the wild instant of a poem,
and there they remain, still, forevermore,
Soul and Idea.

Delirium

You saw me once…
So on the search,
Knowing delirium
Is yours already,
In search of green eyes,
Conceiving a memory,
And memory in verse,
Verse tonight,
The night in your eyes.
You saw me once,
And so I search.

Images

Images, images,
Her eyes were green
For years, they went through
Things of mine
Without finding her.
Images, images,
Light in her eyes
Shone, maybe,
In the corner of time.
Got lost in her eyes,
Even before touching her,
From there on to dusk
All was green.
Green-eyed creature!
The hymn should've
Reached your ear.
Great voices came out
Of the corner of time
That afternoon
You contemplated silence.
Not knowing of me,
Not flowing from me,
The hymn I would write
To reach your ear.

Where are you now?
Lost in time,
Still, caress reaches,
Makes a sound
Of that hymn written
To reach your ear.

It Must Always
Be There

It must always be there,
The "If you knew,"
That fortunate day
That can't ever be
Found in the horoscope.
It's the neighboring sign
For what you captured,
What sinks in silence
Where rumor doesn't reach,
And there are no secrets.
It's the sign, written,
Closer to the rhythm
Of centuries heavy,
Insistent;
Yesterday's step,
Not yet through,
Reflecting hurry,
Decayed by time.
Leave routine behind.
In its loving,
Let it fill the soul
And the haste of being

Or at least existing.
Inside what ends not,
What you can't see,
What exists in fear
In the waking moment
Of guessing,
The irreparable blow
Of absence.

Old Sun

Where does it end,
the whisper of clearer hours?
You say it, you who've counted
the lines in my hands;
you say it, you who know
my tearless eyes;
you say it, you who guard
my best secrets
and in passing have seen
death and life;
you say it, old sun,
where does it end,
the whisper of my clearer hours?

Tranquility

To search everywhere for what isn't,
to feel the unattainability of the insignificant,
to fill up with what's only mine,
and to do so before many,
many things remembered,
before many things forgotten,
I am the saddened heresiarch;
I am my own sleeplessness invader;
I am the hermit amongst people;
I am the Christians
in the Roman circus;
I am the Jews in the ghettos,
enduring hunger and rejection.
No truce for the chase
of all those century ideas…
Blue!
Never quite reaching you, but watching,
resigning myself to the idea of your distant existence,
nostalgia blue and feverish blue.
Solitude blue and blue delirium,
only you know about the tear,
sadness blue and blue martyrium.
We met here, in this ethereal prison
that came over me with stars and spaces.

Going On

Ever-meandering
path,
made for my hands only,
and so for my eyes,
traced in a corner
on the run, made
without architects or flowers,
that's the way I want you,
ever meandering path;
there where your line follows,
where it ends,
there you will take me,
and I'll say nothing,
path;
made for my strength only,
that's the way I want you,
ever meandering.

Blindness

Love is the soul of genius,
And my god is the god of the blind.
I made all those lights they know,
And from one of those sprang the shadows.
I love all light.
I love all shade.
I love all universes untouched by my light.
I, too, love horizons my blood doesn't bathe.
I even love the man who killed my father.
Bird, I know you fly,
Mad from color and music,
As I am mad from dreaming too much.
Poor flightless things!
Poor bloodless things!
Bird, we'll go together,
For I know how to fly too;
I'll cover all suns with the wings of a phoenix,
And one millennium's worth of shadows
will enter your eyes.
The lights on the path don't matter;
Our god is the god of the blind;
Our god is the God of all gods.

Unedited Poem About Hidden Ideas

Kindness opens the door
of Man,
not intelligence
or wealth,
and so their nobleness
begins
as it ends,
in the impious, cruel,
and corrupt monarch;
that's the way he tarnishes his throne,
in lightness and vice,
he who decrees the entrance
to the awakening of Man
and the honor of the sword
that exalts the world.
We all fit there;
we all fit there,
even those who dream
of owning a house
and not an empire

to regulate time
and wander the world,
the skeletal early riser,
light of the Universe.
So I'll say it myself:
*"Por esta, que es mi raza,
ha de hablar el Espíritu."*[74]
I'll say it today:
"También soy Español!"[75]

---

[74] For this, my kin, must the Spirit speak.

[75] I'm Spanish too.

AI[76]

You aren't born a poet;
inspiration must be passed
from that very first roar
that sprang the beginning,
the walking of man.
The drive that pushes
to create, the idea
that flows into poem,
reaps its energy
from the very Universe
and not from a wall
with an electrical socket,
without which you can't think,
you can't, you don't figure
or predict the shot.
Is it path or gorge?
Without it, you end up
isolated and empty,
in a dark corner.
For this, we require
talent to emerge
from the first beating

---

[76] Artificial Intelligence.

of the proud mind
that invented the sockets
that keep you alive:
without them, you are planted,
no sun, no breath,
no advantage or step
in the victory march
nor in failure.
How will you escape
the dark corner
that fills your existence
if you feel no pain,
harbor no hope,
know no sign
in no verse
where man shelters
passion, tenderness,
infinite longing,
search, and mystery,
partner in eternity
and praiser of oblivionless
dreams?

This Day; This Night
October 1987

To my beautiful children

Between the now and the always,
there is a path of light
that I want you to keep,
that I want you to know
and hide between your fingers,
and forge between your wishes,
like the sword of the conscience
that allows you to reap.
There is no more than silence
between the now and the always,
between your voice and mine;
yet, straight like the truth,
it will fill your lone hours
and will tell you in its secret
that it gave you its sign.
Do not break, do not faint
at the reins of a dream;
there is a path of light
that is not what it seems;

so bring your sword, your sign.
Between the now and the always,
what is left is behind;
what is yours, at your side;
what is truth, in your tomb.

Epilogue

Doctor David Zajd, an intellectual from Argentina and medical professor in New Jersey's College of Medicine and Dentistry, once expressed in a conference a statement that should be chiseled in stone: "He who enters as a thief into the life of a nation, stays a thief." That maxim applies to the three ex-presidents of la República de El Salvador: three little thieves, or *mañosos*, as we call them here.

Together, they plundered a ridiculous amount of money (two billion dollars) from the national treasury. One of them is in prison, paying his debt to the people. The remaining two fled to a neighboring country and bought their citizenship there.

The history of the nation must be written, although a void will always linger in the years those men governed. An empty page is better than a list of those corrupt names that showed a fabulous capability for committing the most abject crimes against their own people. "There's nothing more despicable than stealing from poor townsfolk."

But these "ex-presidents" did. So let the two that ran remain far away with their cynical smiles and *dinerito*. They will never again breathe the aroma of their nation; they can't ever say that they walked their people down a path of prosperity.

From now on and until the end of their days, the nation will base its steps on Truth. Only Truth.

Negativity

*Clearing up some things for those who believe
they are being referenced in this book.*

Every situation alluded to in this piece of fiction is a product of the author's imagination and inspiration. If you are a good person who helps the weak and the poor, who looks for justice in the corners of life, I'm sure the greatness of your name and your soul won't fit into these pages. I congratulate you, and I hope someday I can shake your kind hand.

But if you are an evildoer who preys on the weak, are easy to bribe to break the law in favor of your buyer, a master of enriching yourself with lies, arrogant and unaware of the clamor that comes from those who suffer, you deserve none of the written beauty of this book.

Stay in the dark corner you call home, and if you are ever able to escape your cowardice, put on a clean shirt, and begin by walking the path of compensation and reconciliation so those you've wronged can forgive you. But don't expect them to shake your evil hand. Anyway, I do thank you, too, for reading this piece.

Renato Bettio

About the Author

Roberto Arévalo Araujo MD, FACP, (Renato Bettio) was born in El Salvador. After high school, he traveled to Mexico to continue his studies and was certified as a physician and surgeon by the Facultad de Medicina of the UNAM in Mexico City, 1970. He then interned in the Oakwood Hospital (Dearborn, Michigan), followed by two years in internal medicine at the University of Medicine and Dentistry of New Jersey (UMDNJ). In the three following years, he specialized in hematology and oncology at UMDNJ. He is board certified in internal medicine, hematology and medical oncology.

He is a fellow of the American College of Physicians and the founder of the Cancer and Hematology Center in Pasco and Pinellas Counties, Florida, where they offer radiotherapy, chemotherapy, and immunotherapy. He is also a founder of the Medical Mission of Mercy / Medical

Mission International, whose objective is to freely offer surgical and ophthalmological help to homeless people in El Salvador. In 2002, the mission was nominated for a Nobel Peace Prize.

Now, he offers, dear reader, a bit of the inspiration that his soul embraces, telling stories of impunity and misery, and how they affect the lives of his Central American compatriots. And yet he still ascribes to the belief that the poor's faith, those who have remained, those whose love for life can't be extinguished, those who, above suffering, have a life-affirming philosophy, in spite of it all, that it is better to be here.

Now, he brings to you, dear reader, a piece of the inspiration his soul embraces. He writes stories about impunity and misery that affect his Central American fellow countrymen. Yet he also ascribes himself to the tangible faith of those affected. In them, in spite of their suffering, the longing for life doesn't go out; they have a philosophy that keeps them thinking that it's better to be.

Book of Omens
ISBN Paperback: 978-1-63765-625-9
Paperback Price: $14.95
Page Count: 126

www.ingramcontent.com/pod-product-compliance
Lightning Source LLC
Chambersburg PA
CBHW070310040726
47501CB00018B/1373